HEAVEN'S CASTING ROOM

A NOVEL BY:

ROBERT S. DINNING

First printing – December 2009

DreamCatcher Publishing acknowledges the support of the Province of New Brunswick.

Library and Archives Canada Cataloguing in Publication

Dinning, Robert S., 1974-
Heaven's Casting Room / Robert S. Dinning.

ISBN 978-0-9810721-7-3

PS8607.I56H43 2009 C813'.6 C2009-906072-8

Printed and Bound in Canada using recycled paper.

Typesetter: Michel Plourde

Cover Design: Michel Plourde

55 Canterbury St, Suite 8
Saint John, NB Canada
E2L 2C6
Tel: 506-632-4008
Fax: 506-632-4009
dreamcatcherpub@nb.aibn.com
www.dreamcatcherpublishing.ca

For Patti - thanks for all of your help. Live your story well!

RJ K

This novel is dedicated to my mom and dad, who never stopped believing in my ability to write. To my brother who helped to bring three little angels into this world; and most of all to Tina, who showed me that growing up is not the end of the tale, it is merely the beginning. Thank you for sharing this role with me, if only for the briefest of time.
-Robert S. Dinning
October 2008

ACKNOWLEDGEMENTS

It seems almost surreal as I sit here, trying to remind myself that I am not dreaming, and this is actually my novel, bound, published and ready for people to enjoy. I wanted to create something special that would bring hope to the world, and I believe the result was beyond all my expectations.

It has been a long journey, but after eighteen years of searching, I was fortunate enough to find a publisher who believed enough in my abilities as a writer to give me the chance I had been waiting for. It is for that reason that I would like to thank Elizabeth Margaris, my publisher and friend, who through a sheer force of will has demonstrated what true strength and courage are.

I would also like to acknowledge the contributions of those people who were kind enough to read my stories, through their many incarnations, and whose opinions helped me create a better story. Thanks to Mom, Dad, Cheryl, Nita, Cathy and especially Amy, my Psyche, who saved me in more ways than I can mention.

Live your stories well.

Robert S. Dinning
July 2009

ACT ONE

The doors of the bus swung open and Balthazar tentatively stepped down on to a patch of soft, lush lawn. The blades of grass tickled the bottoms of his feet and the bright sunlight enveloped his naked form with gentle warmth.

He had no memory of where he came from, but he knew that this was the place he should be. Stretching out before him was a large, open concept, wooden building with thick columns that held up a bevelled roof. Around the edges of the building and continuing inside were rows upon rows of circular tables with four oversized, stuffed chairs surrounding each of them. A small, picket fence that was stained the same rich cherry as the columns, ran around the entire length of the property.

Everywhere he looked there were people drinking something from enormous mugs while flipping through tightly bound stacks of paper. Every once in a while he would see somebody put down whatever it was they were reading, smile and then dissipate before his eyes. Likewise, a table could be empty and then suddenly have somebody appear beside it looking confused and scared. Immediately someone with wings would show up and direct them to sit so they could talk.

The building was buzzing with activity and he had no idea what he was doing or whom he was waiting for, so he decided it would be better if he just watched for a while. He was about to sit down on the grass when he saw a bright ball of bouncing colour bound toward him and yell, "Hello! Welcome to the Casting Room!"

The person was neither young nor old and had a perfectly styled mop of dark hair that hung past their shoulders and softly framed a smooth, delicate, porcelain-like, androgynous face.

Balthazar held out his hand and introduced himself to the stranger, "I'm Balthazar."

The person extended an exquisitely manicured hand and grasped his in a deceptively strong grip and said, "It's a pleasure to meet you Balthy. Do you mind if I call you Balthy? It would take too long to have you try and wrap your tongue around my real name, so you can call me Tim. I'm the angel of Death, Greetings and Producer extraordinaire"

Bal smiled, released Tim's hand and said, "It's a pleasure to meet you, Tim. But where are we?"

Tim smiled back and replied, "Oh, its had so many names over the years. Elysium, Valhalla, Heaven, take your pick. It's all those things and a great place for a cup of coffee and a piece of my award winning quiche. It's to die for - literally! I'm so bad!"

Balthazar stared blankly at the multi-coloured clad, bundle of energy in front of him and did not know how to say that he had no idea what he was talking about.

He must have looked especially confused because Tim shook his head knowingly and said, "I'm so sorry, I forgot you just arrived and probably have no idea what I am talking about. But don't worry about it; everything will be taken care of shortly. Now where are my manners? Let's get you some clothes and get you settled in. Please come with me."

Tim turned and bounced away, while Bal took a deep breath and followed him into the building.

Several people at nearby tables paused their reading for a moment and smiled warmly at them as they passed by, and Bal did his best to acknowledge their greeting. Tim bounded to a stop beside one of the pillars and pulled out a notepad and pencil and began to rapidly scribble notes to himself.

"You are a big boy, aren't you Balthy?" stated Tim, eyes flicking over his naked form. "I'm sure I can find something for you to fit in. I'm thinking something in a tangerine."

"Tangerine?" asked Balthazar, "Isn't that a fruit?"

"Of course it is! You are so silly. But it is also the hottest colour of the season, everyone, and I mean *everyone* is wearing it," Tim paused and whispered behind his hand, "It's really big amongst the arch-angels, but don't tell anyone; it would ruin their image!"

Tim puffed out his chest and mocked, "Oh, look at me. I'm a big, bad arch-angel. I like to fight and keep everything safe, but I never have the time to moisturize or use product in my hair."

"Should you be making fun of them?" asked Balthazar, eyes nervously scouring the sky for the imminent appearance of the legendary warriors.

Tim waived his hand dismissively and said, "I would not worry about Mikey and the boys, they know I'm right. Besides as you can see from that picture on the pillar, I was once one of them until I discovered the joys of a bath house and spa."

Balthazar walked up to the ornately framed picture for a closer look, and sure enough, there was Tim, surrounded on all sides by the largest, toughest looking men he had ever seen. Everyone was dressed in full golden armour over flowing white robes, and had shields and great, flaming swords resting at their side.

"I don't know what I was thinking," said Tim as he appeared beside Balthazar with a handful of colourful clothes, "I mean look how pale I was. I should have at least edged my robe in a tasteful teal or luscious lavender, anything to create the illusion of symmetry in the outfit. Oh well! Live and learn I always say. Here you go, put these on and then join me at the table over there for a cappuccino and a piece of quiche."

"Thanks," said Bal, slipping easily into the silky material, "But what is quiche? And why would I want to drink a cappuccino?"

Tim stopped in mid-stride, turned around with his hand on his chest and gasped, "What are they? Only the stuff of dreams my dear boy! I make every quiche by hand with only the freshest, lightest ingredients and it literally melts in your mouth! And a cappuccino is the perfect compliment to it, especially if it is sprinkled with some chocolate and a bit of cinnamon. It is so deliciously creamy and frothy that you will definitely believe you are in heaven."

"It sounds delicious, but what is chocolate?"

Tim let out a little high pitched squeak, placed the back of his hand against his forehead and collapsed into one of the nearby chairs. He fanned himself with his other hand and mumbled, "He doesn't know what chocolate is. What am I going to do with him? How can I explain things he has never experienced? I need an apple martini."

"Are you alright?" asked Balthazar as he sat down in the chair directly across from Tim.

Tim took a deep breath, leaned forward and gently patted Bal's hand, "I'll be fine. I just was not expecting how new you actually are. That's all."

"I don't know if I am new or not," said Bal, "I don't remember anything before I stepped off the bus a few minutes ago. I'm not sure who I am or how things work, but your offer of something to eat and drink sounds like a great place to start."

"I agree. Please dig in,"

Tim waived his hand and instantly a large slice of perfectly cooked quiche and a huge mug of frothy, caffeinated creaminess appeared before

Bal. He picked up his fork and tentatively broke off a small piece of quiche and placed it in his mouth. The sensation was unlike anything he had ever known and as he chewed, the fluffy texture made him groan with appreciation. Next he picked up the mug with both hands and took a long draught. The warm liquid shot down his throat and sent a shiver of pure pleasure pulsating down his spine.

"How are they?" asked Tim.

Balthazar looked in amazement at Tim and raved, "Incredible. Is everything else as good as this?"

"Yes. This is just the beginning of everything. You will experience first hand the highest highs and lowest lows that make up life. You will see and feel such wonderful things; things you cannot even begin to imagine. The vivid colours of all the seasons, the warm glow of a setting sun and the cool touch of a summer breeze on your skin."

"Wow," said Balthazar who had finished eating and was staring intently at Tim, "I want to know, to experience, everything that you are talking about. Where can I learn about life?"

"It is fairly straight forward," said Tim as he sat back in his chair, crossed his legs and placed his hands on his perfectly creased pants. "Think of everyday life on Earth as a never-ending movie, and each of us play a specific part within the production as a whole. As a new actor, you will be assigned a limited role, or guest appearance on Earth, and depending on how well you perform, you will be offered greater and more influential roles until you may even be able to guide the course of the story itself."

"Who decides the roles?" asked Bal as he sat back in his own chair and played with his bottom lip.

"That would be the head writer. Apparently he has a master plan for everything, but with those white socks and sandals, I'm not sure what to think."

"So if this guy decides whichever role I will play, how will I know about it?"

"Good question," said Tim as he absent mindedly played stared in disgust at a split end he discovered on one ringlet. "Do you see that stack of tightly bound paper several of the people around us are reading? Those are the scripts of their upcoming lives."

"Hold on a minute," said Bal as his brow wrinkled in confusion, "You mean that everyone is aware of everything that will happen to them?"

"Certainly."

"But doesn't that taint the experience? I mean, if they know the outcome of everything before it happens, why take part at all?"

Tim stared in wonder, brushed back his hair and said, "Excellent question Balthy! Very few actors, even the most experienced ones, have ever asked me that. It looks like your first role is going to be something more challenging than average. To answer your question, after you are born, you must choose to forget everything. Only then will you be able to truly embrace the experience and become the role. You will have no memory of this place or who you were before. All you will know is that brief moment in time."

Balthazar shook his head in agreement, but did not say anything.

"When their role is completed, they return here to discuss everything with a producer similar to myself and prepare for their next assignment."

"So how many assignments or roles do we get the chance to experience?"

"That varies," replied Tim, "It depends on the actor's ability to give a realistic performance and what things they learn and thereby take from their roles. Most people generally accept six or seven lifetimes before trying something new. However, after you reach a certain point, not only does it becomes up to you if you want to go back again, but if you do, you can actually help to influence the course of the story itself! I know some people who have been around since the beginning of the story and want to see it through to the end. Personally, I think it makes as much sense as wearing plaid and stripes together because as I have said, the story is never-ending. Hello!"

"So after people are on...where are they again?"

"Earth."

"Earth, right. After they are on Earth, how do they find their way back here?" asked Bal, frowning his brows.

"That's easy. Everyone always knows their way back home, whether they are aware of it or not. Then sometimes, and usually only under extraordinary circumstances, we are permitted to actually go to Earth and escort the person back. But for that privilege, the person would have to be very special. Very special indeed."

"That makes sense. Will I be able to do that someday?"

"Perhaps," said Tim, a strange half smile playing at the corners of his lips. "After all, this is Heaven and anything is possible here."

"What an amazing challenge," said Bal, adjusting himself in the seat,

"How do I go about applying for a part?"

"You just did," replied Tim with a large smile, "Here you go."

Tim waived his perfectly manicured fingers over the table top and suddenly the dishes were gone, replaced with a thin stack of bound paper. Balthazar stared at the script and gently traced the raised, golden letters on its surface.

"Are you ready?"

"I think so."

Balthazar turned to the first page of *The Whore.*

THE WHORE

It was almost Christmas and the city did its best to hide the forgotten masses of humanity beneath the false glitter and decorations that lined the unforgiving streets. One such creature, plastered in thick make-up and cheap perfume, stood with her tiny back pressed against a building and watched people rush by without a glance in her direction.

She felt invisible and alone.

The heat from the grate she stood on provided a brief respite from the plunging temperature around her. The weatherman said it was going to snow that night and she knew that she should be heading home, but she couldn't. She was afraid.

He would be there.

If she were show up without completing a single trick, he would beat her for being lazy and unattractive.

Her dark eyes flicked over the crowd of people and she tried to stand like the models she would watch on television, with her delicate hands resting on newly developing hips. It would have looked a bit comical if it were not so sad; someone so young trying to look so old.

She nervously bit her bottom lip and hoped that someone would notice her.

Someone did.

Suddenly a figure appeared beside her, seemingly out of thin air. He was well dressed in a full length dark overcoat, dark turtleneck and shiny shoes. A black fedora covered his auburn hair and the way the collar of the coat was flipped up caused his face to disappear into shadow. All she could make out was the chisled outline of his face and gleam of his eyes.

Something did not feel right, but she needed the money.

"So, you wanna have some fun?" she asked as she pushed aside the nagging sensation to run.

"Oh yes," replied the man in a slow, deep voice, "I am very interested in having some fun with you."

"OK, come with me. I know a place."

She stepped off the grate and immediately the icy cold of the pavement cut into the soles of her bare feet like knives as she turned into the nearby alley with her trick in tow. They moved about twenty feet down and stopped where the light ended and the darkness began. The strange thing was that she could still see the gleam from his eyes.

"Is here OK with you?" she asked, leaning into the shadows of the wall.

The gentleman looked quickly around and whispered, "Yes, this is perfect for what I have in mind."

Then he smiled; not a smile of kindness, but one born out of malice.

She could tell he was excited.

He licked his lips and slurped, "Now be a good whore and turn around. Let me see what I am paying for."

She did as she was told and turned around and placed her little hands against the dirty bricks of the wall. Their texture was damp and unforgiving, just like every day of her eleven years of life.

She could feel the heat from the gentleman's gloved hands as he hiked up the back of her filthy dress. She closed her eyes and waited.

Suddenly something hit her in the side of the face and little flashes of light danced around in front of her eyes. Her face felt wet and there was a strange taste of copper in her mouth. She found herself on her back in a pile of rags, staring up into the night sky and into the cold eyes of her attacker.

Spittle was running from the corners of his mouth as he raised a gloved hand to hit her again. She tried to cover her face with her arms, but that just seemed to excite him more and he rained blow after blow down upon her skinny form.

She realised that the best thing to do would be to like back and let it happen, but something inside her refused. She started squirming around and tried to scream, but a soft, gloved hand clamped down over her mouth, stifling all sound.

His breathing grew heavier and as he pinned her down beneath his weight, she knew what was coming next.

It wasn't the first time she had been raped.

"I know you want me to fuck you. You'd like that, wouldn't you? So you could infest me with your filth and disease! Things like you repulse me. It is all I can do to stop from retching at your stench."

She managed to free an arm and tried to scratch his eyes out, those shiny, dead eyes, but he quickly pinned it back beneath her.

"Now that wasn't very nice," he whispered and backhanded her across the side of the face. Her head whipped to the side and when she heard something tiny hit the nearby garbage can, she realised it was one of her teeth.

"Now look what you made me do. It would appear that you need to learn a lesson about how to respect your elders."

The blows came fast and furious, but his demeanour never changed. In fact, his breathing never quickened; he remained distant and callously in control.

He was hurting her, but he didn't seem to care.

It was over quickly.

He leaned down and whispered into her ear, "I did not like doing that, but you had to learn. Now would you like your payment?"

She cringed away from the feeling of his hot breath on her icy neck. Her tongue played with her swollen lip as she did her best to stop the flow of tears streaming from her eyes. She then did something her uncle had told her never to do with a client, she looked at him right in the face and locked eyes with him. She knew it could have consequences, but she needed to get paid.

She felt herself being drawn in by their darkness, but she managed to say, "Yes, give me my money."

He smiled benevolently at her and with his gloved hand, gently wiped the tears from her cheeks and said, "I didn't say anything about money."

She felt her stomach drop.

"I said would you like your payment. You see, you are a disgusting, disease ridden whore, and for that you must make amends."

Oh no.

"You must pay for your sins against God. You must pay with your life."

She saw a brief flash of steel and then a deep, penetrating coldness in her side. It suddenly became difficult for her to breathe, almost as if she were trying to do so through pudding.

Somehow the man had risen to his feet without her noticing and was intently staring down at her.

"Don't worry little one, it will all be over soon. Here is something for your trip."

He reached into the front pocket of his overcoat and pulled out two shiny coins.

"These are for the boatman when you see him."

Boatman? There were no rivers or lakes here, it was all concrete and asphalt. The coins hit the pavement beside her and as the man turned to walk away his eyes sparkled and he said, "Merry Christmas."

The cold of the pavement under her back seemed to draw the heat from her frail body. She began to shiver and as she raised her head, she saw steam escaping from her side. Her ragged dress felt wet and the pile of dirty rags beside her were soaked a deep purple.

She breathed a sigh of relief because blood was red, not purple. She could get up and go back to the place she lived. She didn't call it a home because it wasn't. Only one place had ever been a home to her, and that was when she lived in her Nana's house.

Nana was a kindly woman who was always ready with a hug and a giant mug of hot chocolate. There were always such wonderful smells coming from her home and every year, she would help Nana make gingerbread houses and then decorate their walls and roofs with thick layers of chocolate candy.

It was strange, but it was almost as if she could smell the Christmas turkey with all the trimmings. She liked mashed potatoes the best, smothered in home-made gravy, followed by pumpkin pie for dessert. She would eat so much that she could barely move and then they would sit in front of the fire and relax as Nana told them stories about fairies, dragons and unicorns.

Unicorns were her favourite animal and she kept one hidden in her room. Someday she would travel and see Unicorns in the wild. If they let her, she would climb on their backs and ride with them across deep green fields, far away from the dull grey surrounding her. Nana promised her that they would go travelling someday, wherever she wanted to go.

She loved her Nana and her Nana was the only one who ever loved her.

She was eight when her Nana died and she was sent by the court to live with her only living relative, her great uncle Arvid. What they didn't realise, what nobody from the court could foresee, was they had placed an innocent with a monster.

Arvid was a horrid, short, fat, balding man with thick glasses and a disgusting habit of sucking on his false teeth after meals. He smelled terrible and would always lounge around the house in his torn underwear with his legs splayed wide enough for his privates to fall out.

She asked him once why he wasn't wearing pants, and he became angry, smacked her in the mouth and told her that it was his house and he could do whatever he wanted to in it.

Arvid was a mean man. When he wasn't yelling, he was staring at her with his huge eyes and slowly licking his lips. He did not allow her to close the bathroom door when she on the toilet or in the bath and always made her sit on his lap and bounce around every evening before bed.

He would even ask her to reach into the front pocket of his pants and feel around for a shiny new quarter. Once she had even seen his penis when he was sitting in his chair with his bathrobe untied. He saw her stare and told her not to worry because that was the head of the family. She had been too young to understand what was happening, but that ended one autumn evening; as did her childhood.

The memory was hazy and it was difficult for her to remember exactly what had happened, but she knew that it happened several times.

Her uncle had three of his friends over for a game of poker and after she went to bed, she could hear muffled voices and laughter; a lot of laughter. She remembered shivering on the army cot that served as her bed and trying to get warm by cocooning herself in the threadbare, flannel sheet that covered her. There were heavy footsteps in the hallway outside her room and she heard Arvid say, "She's in there."

"And you're sure she's fresh?" asked another voice.

"Yeah, we didn't pay three bills each to dine on leftovers!" chimed in another.

"Oh, she's fresh alright. Nice and firm." replied Arvid.

"And you're certain that no one will know? The last thing I need is for her to tell someone that I've been wearing her as a hat!" questioned a third.

They laughed and Arvid sniggered, "Of course no one will find out. After all, I'm her great uncle! Who would believe that I have anything but her best interests at heart. Who's first?"

"I am!" said a voice and then the door to her tiny bedroom opened up and she could see a silhouette standing in the doorway beside Arvid's fat form.

The rest of the night was a blur.

Arvid took her out of school and she became the "guest of honour" for dinner guests that came by the house several times per week. It wasn't long before she had progressed to photographs and then home movies, all arranged by her uncle.

Once, the police came by because someone had given them a tip about what had been going on, but instead of helping, the officer in question became one of her regulars.

It seemed no one could help her.

She wanted nothing more than to disappear into her Nana's warm embrace because she had always felt safe in her fleshy arms. Nothing could harm her. Each night she would pray that her Nana would come and take her away from the darkness of the world, away from the monsters that lived in it.

But nothing changed.

Each day Arvid would send her out to the street and beat her upon her return if she did not bring back enough money for him. He never remembered her birthday and she never received a single present from him at Christmas.

Years had passed, and if anything, Arvid was becoming meaner. He had taken to hitting her with an orange wrapped in the toe of a sock because that way the bruises would be internal and his merchandise would remain unblemished.

She feared to go home, especially now that she had been hurt. He would be furious that she didn't follow his rules for dealing with tricks on the street, especially during this holiday season. Arvid always told her to get the money from the trick before anything happens and never, under any circumstances, look at them in the eye. It made people feel uncomfortable and her job was to make them want her, plain and simple.

She had broken both of his strictest rules and there was no telling what he would do to her when he found out.

No. She would stay here for a while longer and try to figure out what she would say. Besides, the ground wasn't so cold anymore. In fact, she was starting to feel warm all over, just like when she used to take bubble baths at her Nana's house when she was younger.

She turned her head and looked down the alley toward the bustling street. People rushed along carrying bags of presents for under the tree, oblivious to the dirty child resting on a pile of rags only a few feet away.

The street lights had come on and their bright yellow light illuminated the decorations tied to the poles. Wreaths, snowmen, reindeer, Christmas trees and stars all glowed and sparkled with a life of their own.

She could smell the various foods the street vendors were selling and it made her mouth water and stomach growl. She must be hungry, but she didn't feel it. Even the vehicle sounds seemed to be muffled and getting further away.

Strange.

A gentle breeze circled through the alley and brought with it a few flakes of snow. They floated toward her and disappeared upon touching her nose and face.

The sensation made her laugh and she turned her attention back toward the slice of sky visible between the buildings. Normally the light from the city obscured all of the stars in the night sky, but tonight they shone brighter than she had ever seen before. It was as though the angels had lit candles just for her.

She wished here Nana could see this.

"I can my little one. I can."

She turned her head toward the voice and stared into the kindly eyes of her Nana.

"I'm here to take you home."

Nana smiled warmly and reached down, folding her arms protectively around her granddaughter. She drew her close and kissed her gently on the forehead.

The little girl smiled.

ACT TWO

"Merry Christmas, little one," said Nana, gently smoothing back the hair from the little girl's bloodied face. "I missed you very much."

The little girl felt hot tears running down her face because she knew at last, she would be safe. Her Nana would never let anything bad happen to her.

"I missed you too. I'm not feeling good," she whispered quietly as she buried her face into her Nana's fleshy form.

"I know, pet, I know. But don't be scared, I'm here to take you on a wonderful adventure. I found the unicorns and they would like to meet you."

Her eyes were growing heavy and suddenly she was no longer afraid of the darkness of the city and the monsters that dwelled within it. She felt herself drifting away, as if to sleep, but she still managed to smile slowly and say, "Unicorns? That sounds like fun. Will there be hot chocolate?"

"Yes," said Nana, her voice choking up, "All the hot chocolate you can drink, and I've made a Christmas feast with all the trimmings; even mashed potatoes and gravy."

"I...like mashed...potatoes and gravy...."

"Good, because I made them just for you. It's time to go before the dinner gets cold. Are you ready?"

"Mmm hmm," said the little girl, closing her eyes and snuggling into her Nana.

"All right," said Nana as she embraced the forgotten child from a disposable life, "Hold on tight."

The cold darkness of the alleyway disappeared beneath the warm glow of the overhead stars in the night sky. The little girl felt herself being lifted as easily as the wind would a feather, and drawn upward into the light. It had a brilliance that was radiating, yet comforting. It welcomed her with open arms, and for the first time since her Nana died, she felt happy.

The light flowed past her like the relaxing waters of the Caribbean and she felt herself travelling at an incredible speed. She didn't know where she was going, but instinctively knew that it had to be better than the place she came from.

Time ceased to have any meaning for the little girl. She was floating in what could only be described as pure bliss, and was not in a hurry to leave. Gradually the light receded and she found herself standing beside her Nana on a sea of green grass. The summer sky was a deep blue and fluffy white clouds drifted lazily by on a gentle current of air. A warm breeze caressed her tiny cheek and she closed her eyes to feel the sunlight touch her delicate features.

It had been a long time since she had been in the countryside, and if this was heaven, it was everything she had ever dreamed. There was only one more thing that would make it complete.

"The Unicorns?" asked Nana with a smile.

"Yes," replied the little girl with a shocked expression, "Can you read my mind?"

"Of course," said Nana, her smile broadening, "You can do anything here; even ride a Unicorn. Look over there."

Nana extended a wrinkled finger and pointed behind the little girl, toward a building that had suddenly appeared. It had a nice wooden fence and inside the building there were a lot of people sitting at tables, reading stacks of paper.

"Where? I don't see anything except busy people reading stuff."

"Not those people," said Nana, "Look over there, by the corner of the fence."

The girl's eyes grew large in surprise and she blushed with excitement. Standing by the corner of the fence, staring directly at them with big brown eyes, was the most magnificent creature she had ever seen. It was jet black with a rainbow coloured mane and tail, but the most prolific part of it was the long, solitary, silver horn growing out of its forehead. It was a Unicorn; a real Unicorn.

She looked at her Nana and then sprinted toward the legendary creature, stopping only after throwing her little arms around its neck to give it a big hug. It was warm and soft and smelled like mango tangerine.

"Careful, pet," said her Nana as she joined the little girl beside the Unicorn, "Did you ask him if you could hug him? I think that would be a good idea."

She paused, tilted her head away from his neck and stared into an intelligent brown eye that stared right back at her. "Excuse me," she said, "Do you mind if I give you a hug?"

"Not at all," replied the Unicorn, "In fact, you can give me all the hugs you would like."

The girl shook her head because she could not quite believe what she had heard. "You can talk?"

"Of course I can. Why do you sound so surprised?"

"Because where I come from, horses cannot talk."

"They cannot talk here either, but I am not a horse. I am a Unicorn and my name is Ben. You must be Ember, your Grandmother has told me all about you. I have been looking forward to meeting you for a very long time."

"Really?" asked Ember.

"Absolutely," replied Ben, shaking his head, "I've heard that you are a very special little girl and I would like to take you for a ride and introduce you to some of my friends. That is if it is OK with your Nana."

The little girl looked expectantly at her Nana, who smiled and said, "That's not a problem at all. You can do all the riding you want, but come inside first for a cup of hot chocolate. You've had a long day and you must rest for a while first. Besides, you have forever to explore up here."

"OK," said Ember giving Ben another giant hug, "I will be right back after my hot chocolate."

"I will be nearby," replied Ben as he leaned down and nuzzled her with his giant head.

Nana took the little girl by the hand and led her inside the cafe. They stopped by a large table beside an enormous wooden post and sat down in large, overstuffed chairs that were so big, Ember's feet did not even touch the ground.

"Is this heaven?" asked the little girl.

"Yes it is," replied Nana, "Why do you sound so surprised?"

"Because in Sunday School I was always taught that bad people don't come to heaven, but I'm here."

"Why do you think that you are a bad person, little one?" asked Nana.

"Well," she began quietly, "After you died I lived with Arvid and he was a mean man. He would hurt me and make me do things that I didn't want to. I tried to tell people what happened, but nobody believed me. No one at all."

The little girl was sobbing now as years of anguish came rushing out in the tears that streamed down her face.

"His friends would come over and they would....would....they hurt me. I wanted them to stop, but they didn't listen. All the time Arvid would laugh and call me dirty names, he said that I deserved it; deserved to be used and thrown away like the trash I was. He told me I was a bad person and I believed him. He taught me how to hustle tricks on the street and then beat me every night I came home if I did not make him enough money. It was horrible. He never bought me a birthday present or anything for Christmas, he would just sit in his recliner and make me watch him open his gifts. No one loved me. I was alone. Then tonight I met that bad man on the street who hurt me and told me that I had to pay for my sins against God. I am a bad person, so how can I be here in heaven?"

Nana reached across the table and took Ember's shaking hands in her own. She looked at her only granddaughter and said, "Now you listen to me. You are not a bad person. You are a beautiful, articulate little girl that I love very much. You had a very difficult life, surrounded by bad people that wanted to extinguish the light inside you because it scared them. Those horrible things that happened to you were not your fault, and I don't want you to ever think that they were. And for that man you met tonight, even he played his part because he enabled me to come and get you. You have done nothing wrong, that is why you are here in heaven. You are my granddaughter and there is nothing you could have done to make me think that you are a bad person."

The little girl slowly nodded her head and Nana gave her tiny hands a gentle, reassuring squeeze. "Now drink your hot chocolate before it gets cold."

Ember wiped her eyes with the back of her hands and then picked up the enormous cup of steaming hot chocolate. It smelled thick and rich, and as she took a big mouthful, the liquid raced along her tongue and filled her entire being with flavour and knowledge.

Suddenly he remembered who he was, and as the mug of hot chocolate was placed back on the table, the little girl's frail form had been replaced by that of Balthazar. Sitting across the table from him was a clean shaven, youthful looking man with short, dark, wavy hair and two enormous gold earrings hanging from his earlobes. He was wearing a rainbow coloured dress shirt and had two large, feathery wings erupting from his back.

"Are you OK, Balthy?" asked Tim with concern.

"I don't know," replied Bal, "That was horrible. The things that girl.... that I went through were absolutely horrid. I had no idea that people could be so cruel."

Tim nodded and said, "Yes they can. Humanity can be capable of both the greatest atrocities in history and the most magnificent gestures of kindness. They are a dual creature and we bring whatever side of our persona to the characters we play."

"Are you telling me that what those people did to me was scripted? That someone actually wrote what they would do? I was just a little girl! I didn't know any better! I had the world ahead of me and then some monster came along and changed everything! How can you justify that?"

Tim sighed and nodded his head sadly, "It cannot be justified. What happened to you was unfortunate, but I can assure you that it was not written as it turned out. Actors are responsible for finding their own ways of approaching different situations. Sure, the script had been prepared for their life, but it is always changing as their free will is added to the story. Sometimes unexpected things happen, but everything happens for a reason."

"What kind of reason could there be for people like that?" snarled Bal, clenching his fist on the table. "For people that hurt children? I would love to show them the true meaning of pain and make them understand clearly that their actions deserve an extreme reaction."

"Now Balthy," said Tim, "Try to calm down. Don't give into the rage, you are far too young to be this angry. Remember that everything was part of a story; everyone you met were actors like yourself. They are not bad people, at least they didn't start out that way. Sometimes an actor gets so into their role that they become lost and do not have the ability to find themselves again."

"So what happens to these people? I assume there is a Hell and they are suffering there even as we speak?" muttered Bal, unclenching his fist with a great deal of difficulty. He could feel the anger and resentment burning and bubbling in his chest like a wild creature. It was a new sensation for him, but one which he instantly liked. He took a deep breath and forced the beast down, down inside his very core where he locked it away.

Tim took a deep breath and said, "There is a place for people who have lost themselves, but it is not what you think it is. The term Hell was coined by the Romans and referred to a burning garbage pit at the edge of their cities. So when people were threatened with the possibility of being thrown into the burning pit of Hell unless they lead a good life, they took it to heart and it became metaphysical rather than literal."

"So Hell is not real?" questioned Balthazar, the fire in his belly slowly cooling.

"It was definitely real, but it is an earthly concept. What exists here is different and I truly hope you never find yourself in a position to experience it."

"Fine. But will all my roles be as horrible as that last one?" asked Bal with the barest hint of a snarl in his voice.

"No, not at all," replied Tim, relieved that Balthazar seemed to be calming down. "Every role is different and unique. As you have experienced first hand, sometimes you could be male, other times female, it all depends on the role you are assigned."

"So basically anyone can be anyone at any point in time."

"Exactly."

"So when am I eligible for another role?" asked Bal. "I want to try again."

Tim shrugged his shoulders and said, "That I am not certain of. You could be assigned another script immediately, or have to wait until something becomes available. It's really all in the hands of the casting director."

"Fine," said Bal, leaning back in his chair, "I can wait. By the way, wasn't your hair a lot longer the last time I saw you?"

"It was! Thanks for noticing! I was growing bored of it and thought it was time to mix things up a bit. I know it is a bit drastic, but do you like it?"

Bal felt himself finally relax and he smiled and said, "I do. It makes you look younger, and the earrings really set everything off."

"Oh behave!" chided Tim, blushing with the compliment, "Don't you know that flattery will get you everywhere!"

"Speaking of everywhere, where did Ben go? I still would love to go for a ride."

"I'm sure he is around here somewhere. He's probably finding a saddle to wear that matches his mane - he is a bit vain like that."

"Really?"

"Oh yes! Don't get me started!" laughed Tim.

"I'm amazed that he was that friendly," said Bal, "I don't know if I would be that friendly after being mounted by someone and ridden hard all day. Would you?"

"Hmmm," replied Tim, lost in thought. He was about to reply when the smell of cinnamon wafted through the cafe.

Bal turned as the most magnificent woman he had ever seen strolled effortlessly into the Cafe. She was tall, voluptuous and confident. Her thick mane of red, curly hair accented her alabaster skin and gave her the appearance of a living statue. She was dressed in a tight, blue dress that was cut so high and low that it barely left anything to the imagination. But the most prominent feature on her entire body was the pair of raven black wings on her back.

She was magnificent.

Powerful green eyes locked with his and he felt himself powerless in their embrace as she floated across the room to stand in front of their table. Tim's eyes flicked uninterestedly over her and he said, "I thought I smelled something cheap. Hello Elley."

Elley momentarily took her eyes away from Balthazar and quipped, "Oh, hello Tim. I see that time has not been kind to you. Just remember that you are supposed to chew your hotdogs."

Tim smirked and said, "Cute. So, what do you want?"

"Nothing much. I just thought I would come by and introduce myself to this magnificent piece of man meat," replied Elley as she stared at Balthazar in much the same way as a shark would look at its next meal.

Tim sighed, rolled his had and said, "Balthazar, this, uh. lady is Elley. Elley, this is Balthazar."

Balthazar stood up and extended his hand. Elley's eyes flicked over Bal's muscular form before she grasped his hand and commented, "My, you are a big boy, aren't you? I'm Dana Eleonora Veronica Isabella Linda, but you can call me Elley."

"It is a pleasure to meet you, Elley," said Balthazar, gently shaking her hand.

"I can certainly hope so," whispered Elley, locking eyes again with Bal, "And what are you gentlemen discussing?"

"Balthy has just returned from his very first role and he was curious if every other time it will be that hard."

"I like things when they are hard," said Elley, her eyes never leaving Bal's.

"Believe me, everyone knows that!" sniggered Tim.

Elley shot Tim a venomous glance and Tim merely smiled and blew her a kiss.

"Anyway," sighed Elley, "I would love to stay and pump you for information all day, but I'm on a rather busy schedule. Time's tight."

Tim leaned toward Balthazar and said behind his hand, yet loud enough for Elley to hear, "That's the only thing."

Elley ignored the comment and continued, "Perhaps we can meet again when you have some spare time. Do you ride well?"

Bal shrugged his shoulders and said, "I guess so. But where will we find horses?"

"Who said anything about horses?"

Bal felt his face grow red and was about to comment when Tim's gagging sounds distracted him. Elley pursed her lips in frustration and said, "I'll keep my eye on you, Balthazar. I think you have a huge future with us. Take care."

"Buh bye!" said Tim as Elley turned and walked away.

"She seems like a nice lady," said Bal as he watched her leave, hypnotised by her bum; it looked like two puppies gently playing under a blanket.

"She certainly is something. Suddenly I feel the need to shower."

"Does she work with you?"

Tim's entire demeanour shifted and he said in a serious tone, "No, she definitely does not work with me, or anyone else in this room."

"I'm confused," said Balthazar, suddenly concerned by Tim's change in mood. "If she doesn't work with you, what does she mean that I have a huge future with her?"

Tim stroked his chin thoughtfully for a moment before continuing, "Elley is talent scout for our rivals. They own their own studio and have a pool of actors that interact with our actors on earth."

"In the same story?"

"Yes, and no. See, every actor is limited by the story itself, but within that story, various actors can chose what they want to do, which path they want to follow. It's not necessarily existentialism versus fatalism, they are one in the same; both can exist simultaneously. Do you understand?"

Balthazar shook his head and said, "I have no idea what you just said. I will just take you at your word that Elley represents another studio that may be interested in signing me."

"That sounds fair," replied Tim, nodding. "But believe me when I say that Elley is not to be trusted. She is a man eater and always has something up her sleeve. Take everything she says with a grain of salt. Does that sound fair?"

Bal stuck out his bottom lip and was about to respond when a script suddenly materialised on the table in front of him.

It was thick and bound together with silver rings. Raised golden letters gleamed on the cover page and Bal knew that it was meant for him.

"That was a lot faster than I expected," said Tim in surprise.

"Not the first time you've heard that, is it Tim?" said a loud voice from a nearby table.

Tim made a dismissive gesture in the direction the voice came from and said, "Ignore them Balthy. They are just bitter, that's all. I think that script is for you."

"I think you're right," responded Bal. "Let's see what they have in store for me this time."

He gently touched the golden lettering with the tips of his fingers and then turned to the first page of *The Professor*.

THE PROFESSOR

OK, so here I am at the age of 30, weighing over 300 pounds, sitting at my old, decrepit typewriter, drinking a large glass of cherry whiskey and coke in the early July evening.

I can't help but wonder, how did I end up here? To tell the truth, I'm not sure what happened. It seems like one minute I am living abroad, hanging out in Cafes, drinking cups of coffee strong enough to chew, in the best shape of my life, and the next, suddenly I find myself in my present gelatinous form, back home, far away from my girlfriend and experiencing rage beyond the next level.

I thought that I had managed to finally accomplish something this year. After four years of sucking the asses of my fellow teachers in a useless attempt to gain their trust and understanding, thereby allowing me the opportunity to slither into the ranks of full time status, I thought I finally succeeded.

It nearly killed me.

I despise all forms of sucking up. There seems to be something incredibly unmasculine about kissing someone's brown eye to gain their support! But, as any of you who know about the world of the part time College teacher will verify, not to act as a human suction cup will dramatically decrease your professional career life. So, I closed my eyes and sucked as no one had ever sucked before.

I stayed late at night, marking the shitty grammatical papers of our future, in order to hand them back as soon as possible to try and coerce the little bastards to rate me highly on the year end student survey; usually to no avail.

I had to pretend not to know various things, in order to make the full timers around me feel wanted and special by helping out one of the new part timers. I can't believe I sat there, day after endless fucking day, listening to their endless dribble about what they used to do when they were younger and in my position! There were several times I actually considered kicking them in the balls just to shut them up! I wanted to staple their old lips together so they would be forced to retire and get the hell out of the academic world.

I'm not asking a lot, really, I'm not! Just retire after you have been at the job for 30 years! But do you think that these walking bags of dust will do me the courtesy of dropping dead and creating open spaces? NO! Instead, I stared in horrific humour at these fuckers trying to get out of their chairs in order to walk to class. Frankly, I'm surprised none of them have fallen and broken a hip yet!

Or even worse are these greedy assholes that retire with full pension from another teaching position in High School, then come to College and take a full time job out of the grasping hands of the part timers! Unbelievable! I can't get over why these people feel the need to continue working; especially with a full pension. Even if they wanted to teach on a part time basis, that would be cool because I could draw on their knowledge and maybe get a full time position. But no, that's not possible! They feel that they deserve ANOTHER full time position.

Deserve? Right, just like they deserve getting rammed up the ass by a fourteen inch schlong! FUCK! Why don't they just retire! I must be asking too much!

Then, when against all odds, I somehow manage to claw an interview from the clenched buttocks of the administration, I find out that it doesn't matter because no matter what I do, no matter how hard I prepare, I am predestined not to get one of the positions because I do not have my PhD! A fucking Doctorate! To teach at college? Unbelievable.

True, in the job description it stated that a PhD was preferred, but who cares? I would prefer to try every move of the Kama Sutra with a porn star, but it doesn't appear to be in the cards, does it?

Four years and over fifty courses I sucked up to those fuckers! Four years! And then they repay my lip service by blatantly slamming me up the ass with their dismissal because I only have my Masters Degree in Creative Writing English!

Only.

I guess it doesn't matter that it came from the highest rated arts college in the United Kingdom and cost me a fortune to complete. If my M.A. is receiving such little respect, it makes me wonder why I even decided to get it. I sure as fuck could have done without the extra tens of thousands of dollars of debt that I incurred while completing that piece of paper that could be used only for toilet paper.

So what do I do? I figure that I have not incurred nearly enough debt completing my M.A., so I try to locate a place that will let me complete my PhD and not interfere with my measly income teaching.

I searched the entire fucking world until I finally found a place in the Untied Kingdom that would accept me. Then it takes me another two years to raise enough capital to offset the horrid international student fees! As soon as I paid them, I had the distinct impression of a really large truck, representing the fist of finance office, being driven up a narrow roadway that was previously only one way, representing my asshole.

It was no where near as pleasant as I had been led to believe!

It makes me wonder what all this is for, it really does. I tried so hard to play the game in academia and put up with all the scraps of classes they sent my way and I did it with a big, fucking smile on my face. I didn't say a bad word about anyone, and what did it get me? Nothing! Not a single thing.

And then I had to stand quietly by and watch as they ignored me and gave the jobs to someone else.

I especially enjoyed how after the second interview, I was told by the Chair that the only reason I was not hired was because the committee was not confident in my competence teaching grammar! That's right, I was called incompetent!

I did not know quite what to say, but I had the distinct urge to leap across the desktop, grab him by his throat and pop his head like a giant pimple.

Then, to add insult to injury, the Chair told me that I should attend the 4 day teacher's training session that is being held next month in a nearby city because, "it might help your application for next year."

Do I have asshole written on my forehead?

I must because I went, got drunk with new hires from twelve other colleges and really did not learn a single thing about teaching. Nothing. What I walked away with was a second place trophy for poker.

How apt.

Second place.

The story of my life!

Then, only a few weeks ago now, all the shit came together in the perfect storm; a shitticane, if you will.

I interviewed for the third time and this time I was ready for their in-depth, useless grammatical questions. Not only had I prepared an "exciting" presentation on subordinating and co-ordinating conjunctions, but I had also created seven additional presentations that covered all aspects of grammar, just in case somebody asked me a question about something obscure. One by one I knocked those bad boys out of the park and I was feeling good about myself.

My mistake.

Right near the end of the interview, one of the members of the panel, a cod-faced looking fucker, looked at me with glassy, unblinking eyes and said, “What is ‘is’ in that example? What part of speech is it?”

My mind went blank. I was expecting unusual questions about sentence fragments and the five ways to correct them or the many uses of the comma, but not something that simple.

I froze and I could not even remember my name. Is! What the flying fuck kind of question is that? As I paused, trying to figure things out, I saw the committee write on their papers.

I was fucked with the same certainty of dropping the soap in the shower of a prison. For the record, I know it is a verb and the third person of “be”, but do you think I could remember it at the time? No. Not at all.

The rest of the interview went off without a hitch, and I actually thought that I would finally be offered a coveted full time position in spite of my minor mistake. I would assume that other people would make mistakes as well.

I didn’t hear from them for a good three months and then word filtered through the grapevine about who was hired and when I discovered I was not one of them, I knew I was in trouble.

I was eventually asked to come into the Chair’s office to discuss the interview, and as soon as I walked through the door I got a queasy feeling in the pit of my stomach, similar to the sensation the day after a night of heavy drinking and spicy food.

The Chair sat behind his desk, staring blankly at me and to his right was a hot redhead from Human Resources. She looked really familiar.

I knew instantly what was about to happen.

I took a seat on an insanely small chair and stared across the table at the man who had a face like a sphincter and the personality to match. His eyes were dead and the wispy goatee on his chin looked remarkably similar to my balls.

The Chair took a breath and said, “I see that your area of expertise is in Literature and Creative Writing.”

“That’s correct.”

“But we feel that you are not strong enough grammatically to teach at the College level, and as such, we are severing our relationship.”

Severing our relationship? I’ve got something for you to sever right here, bitch! What am I supposed to say to that? Four years of effort and out on my ass, just like that.

I didn't know what to say. Everything felt surreal, as if I was not me and was merely watching it happen to somebody else; a third person reading a story. The redhead said nothing, but I am certain I saw a smile curl the corner of her lip.

I actually sat there and weighed my options about hitting him across the face with my chair. There was no security around because he most likely thought I was not a threat to his well being. If only he knew how close he was to consuming steak through a straw for the foreseeable future. If only.

So now I have no idea what the future is going to hold for me. I thought for a brief moment that I finally won and Fate had grown tired of tormenting me.

I thought wrong.

For as long as I can remember, I have never been able to win at this game of life, never! Every time I come close to attaining the coveted ring of accomplishment, I get an extra wide size twenty boot right in the nuts, courtesy of my unseen assailant.

Anyone that has ever been spiked in the nads can attest to the fact that it is not a pleasant experience. I remember getting hit with a soccer ball, hockey puck, tennis ball, Indian rubber ball, fist, foot and an uncooked ear of corn in the balls. Each time I thought I would throw up and I was convinced that the pain could never, ever get any worse; again, I was wrong.

But with each successive blow to my manhood, I always pulled myself back to my feet and fought through the burning pain to continue on. Seriously, if I ever get the chance to repay that fucker, I'm going to take a running start and hoof him in the sack from behind so he looks like a football.

Fucking cock-smoker.

Some people will probably say that I am being "too harsh" or "too emotional" about things, and I should find someone to talk to and sort out all my emotions before I give myself an aneurysm. Well, as far as I am concerned, they can take turns eating my asshole with chocolate syrup!

You know, I think that is the main problem with the world today. Everyone has an opinion about everything and they must share it with people who don't care!

For instance, I really don't give two squirts of piss for what religion you belong to. I'm sure it's nice, but why do they always feel the need to come by my home and tell me that eternal damnation awaits me if I do not convert to their religion? Eternal Damnation? Fuck me! I'm pretty sure that I am already there! Now I'm no theologian, but isn't it a bad sign when all different beliefs believe that they are the only true one? According to my calculations, that means that 99.9% of us are fucked! All I can say is that we might as well enjoy the show on the way to the end, just in case we are not part of that .1%.

That brings up my next point on dying. I do not understand why everyone always gets so upset when some fucker croaks. They are not here anymore, so why do people spend so much money on funerals? As far as I am concerned, they should whip the body on a bonfire in the backyard, roast some hot-dogs and slap the ashes into a shoebox from the brand new pair of running shoes they bought with the insurance money. Or better yet, flush the ashes down the toilet like a goldfish! None of this thousands of dollars on a piece of wood that is going into the ground after only one use; it doesn't make sense to me!

I always thought it would be funny to open a funeral home dedicated to putting the F-U-N back into funeral. I could put shirts on the bodies that said, "Yesterday was the last day of the rest of my life," and place beer along side the body to keep it cold.

I could even come up with different theme rooms. In the Safari Room you could watch your loved ones being eaten by lions or in the Medieval Room you could load their body on a catapult and shoot it toward the graveyard (this one sounds like a blast because if you can get a "hole in one", the funeral would be free!) Just think of the publicity.

I could even train vultures to circle old age homes and follow certain people all day. Can you imagine looking up in the sky and seeing a bald headed vulture circling you? It would be hilarious! I would totally send them after the old geezers in my department in hopes of eliminating them from the schooling equation.

I know what you are asking yourself. You are trying to figure out why I am so bitter toward the world and everyone in it. The answer is quite simple; everyone in the world is an asshole. Think I am over analysing this? Then how do you explain these stupid bastards that decide to take their babies on aeroplanes? These ignorant bastards see nothing wrong with subjecting those around them to the incessant screaming of a toddler! They are oblivious to the fact that perhaps others do not want to experience the bliss of a pair of screeching lungs at ten thousand feet!

Then they look at you and snippily state that they paid for the tickets and have every right to be there. Fine. Then I have the right to pick up the little weasels and fold them like a fucking accordion!

Or how about those old people who drive under the speed limit in the passing lane, and no matter what you do, they will not change lanes! You have to slam on your brakes to avoid slamming into their ass end, which causes your delicious coffee to spill out of the hole in the plastic lid and land directly on your crotch, par boiling your family jewels! You curse and communicate your displeasure with non-verbal communication, but they have no idea what is going on and decide to slow down even more because they do not understand why you are so far up their ass that you could give them a prostate exam! Then, by some unknown miracle, their blinker goes on and you think that you can finally get past this future worm buffet. But does anything happen? No! Of course not!

Then you have those precocious little bastards of children that seem to believe they have a right to question your integrity in the classroom. They want you to justify every mark you give them and if they do not agree, they will go and talk to your boss about how unfair and unprofessional you treat them. True, there have been quite a few times when I secretly hoped to go back in time to the night of their conception and tell their fathers to pull out or their mothers to swallow, but I cannot blame them entirely because they know no better.

Rather, I blame the parents who did not put a boot to their children's assess when they were younger, opting instead for discussion and time outs. Why the fuck would you ask your children to explain their reasons for drawing on your new white couch or kicking their sibling in the face? Yeah, a time out or taking away one of their ten computer games will really make them think about not doing it again!

Smack their ass!

Teach them that for every inappropriate action, there will be an immediate reaction. It is not difficult! I was spanked with open hands, wooden spoons, plastic spatulas and even leather belts, and I grew up extremely well adjusted. True, I am exceptionally bitter, but I know the difference between right and wrong. I've seen programs that say you shouldn't hit your kids because it causes them to fear you rather than respect you as an individual. Do you know what I have to say to that? Good! Let them fear me, I have no problem with that! At least they will be respectful of adults.

I'm certain that some people will scream about children's rights and how it is illegal to smack your children; well, I've got some news for you: Fuck off! According to the Supreme Court, it is legal to spank your children as long as "it is done with love". Don't believe me? Check it out for yourself. If I ever have kids of my own, I will so use that to my advantage. I just have to remember to tell them that I love them as I turn their ass scarlet from my hand.

That reminds me, I had to go and see this quack calling himself a doctor the other day because I blew out my asshole and I needed something to dull the pain. Let me tell you, I've never experienced anything like that before. I've always heard women bitching about how men could never understand the pain involved in child birth unless they were to give birth through their asshole. Well, guess what? I've experience it first hand, and I have to say that the sensation was so intense that I actually longed to get kicked in the balls with a frozen boot to help take my mind off things!

As soon as I sat down I knew something was wrong; there was no way that hard, tennis ball shaped turd was exiting my rectum without taking most of my insides with it.

I should have immediately stopped and eaten some of my mother's home-made muffins, which while tasty, were like Drano for your intestines. But, like a fool I decided to continue. My mistake.

There is something incredibly wrong about getting a shit half way down and having it get jammed in there tighter than an extra small thong on an extra large woman. My sphincter was straining, but that bad boy just wouldn't co-operate.

I won't bore you with the details, not because I am concerned by your delicate sense of appropriateness, but for the simple reason that I am trying hard to forget about it. All I will mention about the experience is that for the last few days, everytime I take a power dump it feels like I'm trying to pass a prickly pear that has been coated in hot sauce. Not pleasant.

Anyway, this tool of a doctor takes one look at me and tells me that I need to lose weight because I am a prime target for a heart attack. So I tell this bald fucker that he is a prime target for a toupee.

Can you imagine? Me? A heart attack? Fuck him! I'm only 30 years old. I don't need to worry about that until I'm in my sixties.

So then cock-head, as I now call him, tells me that I need to get my anger in check because my blood pressure is far too high. Too high?

I wonder why. I don't suppose it has anything to do dealing with this asshole who gives me advice about stuff that is none of his business, when all I want is something to take this constant throbbing in my rectum away.

I'm not asking for much, just some extra strength stuff to make me feel like I am looking at myself through somebody else's eyes. Then do you know what this walking phallice suggested? He wanted me to go to the drug store and buy some suppositories to jam up my ass!

I told him he could jam the clipboard up his ass with a twist and left the office.

Rage issues? I don't think so. I do not have rage, I just get very upset when I am surrounded by assholes and people who put up with those very same assholes! I will never understand why people allow others to behave in such an inappropriate manner.

At least it is a beautiful day outside and I can try and relax with cherry whiskey and coke as I pound the keys on this typewriter. The problem is that the more I think about how I got screwed over, the angrier I become.

Those jobs were mine for the taking. I worked hard at it. I deserved one of them. Now with budget cut backs, there is a great chance I will not be able to teach in the fall. Great. All my ass-sucking was for nothing. That is just not right. I've put in my dues; I've paid the price of living on part-time hours with my health and now they are basically saying that I am good enough to graciously eat whatever scraps they throw me, but I am not good enough to get full time employment.

Now my stomach is upset. I'm burping acid and this therapy of writing stuff down is not helping in the least! Even my breathing is getting faster and my right fingertips are going numb from all this typing. Fuck, I need a break. I think I will go and lay down for a while and see if it will help me relax.

ACT THREE

"Where the fuck am I? What the fuck am I doing here?" he said with alarm as he stared at the beautifully carved building that suddenly appeared before him. The sky was a deep blue, and though he could not see the sun, he could feel its light warming his skin.

The smell of freshly made cinnamon buns and home-made bread wafted out of the building and wrapped itself around his senses. He closed his eyes and took a deep breath.

Memories of his childhood in his mother's kitchen came rushing back to him and he realised it was the first time in many decades that he had thought of it. Even though he was not quite tall enough to see over the countertop, he would spend hours watching her cook such wonderful things. He always wanted to help, so it was his job to break open the eggs and whip them up in an old green ceramic mixing bowl for his mom to use.

They never had a lot of money, so his mother would make everything by hand. From bread to butter and even birthday cakes, she could make them all. One of his favourite things was the bunny cakes she would make him for his birthday, complete with chocolate eyes and liquorice whiskers. It was amazing, and she would make smaller versions for the kids he invited to take home rather than a goody bag full of useless toys.

One Easter they had tried to make home-made chocolate cream eggs, and even though they did not turn out that well, it was a lot of fun trying things out. That had always been their motto and he had tried to live that way, he really had.

For years he had tried to play by the rules, only to see those who did not deserve it get ahead in life while he was left behind. Slowly the anger built up inside him until now he could feel a giant knot in the centre of his chest, pressing to get out; to be released. He had done his best to keep a certain perspective on things, always convinced that things had to get better. After all, what kind of loser did the universe think he was? But now the pressure inside him felt like a bottle of fizzy soda pop and he knew that it was just a matter of time before it exploded.

Maybe he needed a change in scenery. Yes, that could be exactly what he needed. Perhaps he would look into travelling somewhere, maybe the Highlands of Scotland or back to Scandinavia. He had been stationary far too long and putting some distance between himself and his present life should help give some perspective to things. The first thing he would have to do is start working out again and burn off some of this extra rage before it killed him.

"I'm sorry Balthy," said a familiar voice, "But it is too late."

He opened up his eyes and standing directly in front of him was the most unique looking person he had ever seen.

"Who the fuck are you? And why are you in my dream?"

The figure smiled warmly and said, "Such anger! You need to relax. Here, come in and try a delicious herbal tea. It will help calm you down."

Tim beckoned him to come inside the gate and pointed toward a nearby, empty table that also seemed very familiar. He followed Tim's lead and moved toward the table, but before he sat down, he felt the familiar surge of rage wash over him.

He snarled, "Calm down? Me? Well since you put it that way, no! Fuck you! I want to know what is going on! The last thing I remembered, I went to bed to try and sleep off some of this stress I was under and then bam! I'm standing here, being offered herbal fucking tea from somebody in a shiny purple shirt!"

"Thanks for noticing, but it's not just purple, it's oberjean. You can tell from the richness of the colour. Would you like to touch it?" asked Tim, extending his arm.

"No! I don't want to touch it or you! I really don't care about the correct colour definition of your shirt either! I just want to know what the fuck is going on! This is not a difficult question. It's not like I'm trying to find out the secret of the pyramids or anything like that."

"Oh, that's easy. Just go and talk with Cleo over there," said Tim, referring to a person sitting by herself at a back table reading something, "She can tell you all about it. And just between you and me, it's nothing like you would expect. I was so shocked that my hair straightened itself! It saved me a fortune at the salon."

"What?"

Tim flicked his long, curly hair back from his face, absent mindedly stroked his neatly trimmed chin length beard and said, "I know it is hard to believe, but this is not natural. I had straight hair since before the Babylonians, but after a few millennia I was bored and decided to try something different. So with the expertise of Maurice in the salon, we opted for something crazy."

"Babylonians? Salon? What the fuck? Am I dead or something?"

Tim paused in mid flourish and said, "Yes, completely. All that anger finished you quicker than one of Michael's cocktails. That reminds me, I should give him a quick ring to see if the party is still on for Wednesday. Anyway, have a seat and I will be right back with your drink."

His head began to swim as he reluctantly sat down in one of the chairs. It was comfortable, but it didn't help soften the blow that he may really be dead. Then a thought hit him and he scowled. What if there was nothing wrong with him and his so called buddies were just having a joke at his expense? But as quickly as the thought entered his mind, it left as another angel walked by.

"Well aren't you pleasant," said a voice from the table beside him.

"What the fuck is it to you?" he replied, not bothering to turn toward the voice.

"Oh, and such an expansive vocabulary! There is obviously no doubt about your level of intelligence. Here, let me see if I can find a ball for you to play with."

He couldn't believe what he was hearing. Someone was trying to talk down to him here, in his own afterlife. He had enough of it when he was alive and was not about to put up with it when he was dead. His bottom lip flicked in and out for a moment, like the tongue of a snake and then he whipped his head around to see who would dare make fun of him.

Sitting at a table to his right was a woman with blond hair and brown eyes, wearing a long, flowing white gown that seemed to shimmer with a light unto itself.

Their eyes locked.

Time stopped.

He disliked her immediately.

He shook his head and said, "Excuse me? What did you say to me?"

The woman smirked and said in a very loud, exaggerated way, "I said, let me see if I can find a ball for you to play with. But then again, maybe the bounce is a little too advanced for you."

"I got your ball right here," he said, motioning below the table.

"I'm sure you do," she replied, "But somehow I doubt that it is impressive at all. But don't worry, I'm sure it is just because it is cold in the cafe."

He was shocked. In all of his thirty years, no one had dared speak to him like that. No one. She reminded him of a mongoose; little and vicious. But what she didn't realise is that he was the snake to her mongoose and he was going to have that rodent for dinner.

He held up his finger and was about to tear a strip off her when Tim reappeared with a large cup of herbal tea and placed it on the table in front of him.

"Here you go, Balthy, drink up! It's my special blend, complete with my secret ingredient. You should find that it adds an entirely new dimension to the flavour."

He paused, gave her a dirty look and then said to Tim, "Look, dude, I don't know who you think I am, but I am not this Balthy guy you keep talking about. I think you have me confused with someone else. I'm sure this tea is delicious, but I am in the middle of something right now."

Tim gave a knowing smile and said, "Oh yes, I see you have met one of our other rising stars. Her name is Cera and she is an excellent actress, though she can be somewhat strong willed."

"That's one way of putting it. I, on the other hand, would call her a b..."

"Now Balthy," interrupted Tim, "Be nice. After all, we are in Heaven."

"But she started it!"

"Never mind. Besides, if you two keep arguing, you are going to stress me out and then Maurice will truly have his work cut out for him. That won't make him happy, and believe me when I say that he can get ugly when he is not happy. The last time it happened, he locked himself in his office and refused to come out for hours."

He raised his left eyebrow and muttered, "Sure man, whatever. She's a pain in my ass and I'm certain that the only thing rising about her will be her skirt in the director's office."

"Balthy," warned Tim.

"OK, fine," he said, turning his attention back to Tim, but not before shooting Cera one last dirty look, which was immediately returned. "So fill me in on what happened to me back on Earth."

"Well," began Tim as he sat down in the large chair across from him and crossed his legs, "It is just like I said earlier. All that anger you carried around inside put such a strain on your heart that it finally exploded just after you went to bed. Do you remember how your right side was getting all tingly while you were typing at your typewriter?"

He nodded and picked up the cup of tea.

"Well, that was the first sign that you were having a stroke. Even if you had called an ambulance, it would not have helped. You were too far gone and your role was up.'

"Role?"

"Yes, role. You see, we are all merely actors in someone else's play. We are assigned certain roles within that play, and even though our time upon the stage of life is short, we gain valuable insight into ourselves with each successive role."

"Successive roles? Are you telling me that I have done more than one role?"

"Exactly."

"Then why can't I remember any of them?" he asked, bringing the cup to his lips.

"Because each role can be so different and so full of its own unique challenges and rewards, that the only way to make the most of it is to choose to forget everything from before. Sometimes it is for the best, especially if you had a particularly challenging role, much like yourself."

He was about to ask Tim what he was talking about when he took a sip of the hot liquid and immediately understood.

He remembered everything. He recalled getting off a bus, Tim's warm greeting, his first life as a little girl and everything that went along with it. But most importantly, he remembered his name.

He blinked, put down the cup of tea and stared at the smiling face of the angel who had guided him through two successive lives. Suddenly he was embarrassed by his behaviour.

"I'm sorry Tim," said Bal, his face flushing with guilt. "I didn't recognise anything or anyone. I shouldn't have spoken to you that way. I really do like that colour of shirt, it looks really comfortable."

Tim's eyes sparkled with warmth as he leaned forward and gently patted the back of his hand with a perfectly moisturised palm.

"You have nothing to apologise for," said Tim, "It must have been such a shock for you to go to bed and then find yourself here. I can't imagine what that must be like. I mean I have gone out places and then woken up in bed, but never vice versa."

Bal rubbed his eyes with the heels of his palms and said, "Yes, it is definitely something that I will never get used to. But I guess it is all part of the job, much like meeting new people."

He turned toward Cera to apologise, but couldn't do it.

He still disliked her.

Bal turned back in his seat and said just loudly enough for her to hear, "Like I said, I'm sorry if I offended *you*."

He could feel Cera's eyes burning into him, but he ignored it which seemed to perturb her more.

"I know this may sound a bit crazy, especially since I have just gotten back, but I was hoping you had another role for me to try. If not, I would be more than happy to just hang out and eat some of your quiche. I tried it back on earth, but something seemed to be missing. It says a lot when I had to die to find something delicious to eat." said Bal with a chuckle.

Tim stared intently at him for a moment, then smiled and said, "As a matter of fact, I do have something that has just arrived hot off the presses. I will be right back with your script Balthy, as well as yours Cera."

He blinked and Tim had vanished, leaving behind the lingering odour of mango tangerine.

"Now don't be scared Balthazar," said Cera, "You are going to see a lot of markings on paper. They are called *words* and those words go together to form something called *sentences*. Now if you take your time, I'm sure that Tim will explain to you what a script is."

Bal gave his biggest, most genuine smile and replied, "While I am certain that you have handled many people's fair share of thick objects, a script is different because you do not swallow it, you read from it. So careful not to strain your mind. You can do it, just sound each word out. Repeat after me, C-A-T, C-AT, CAT. Good girl!"

Cera looked shocked and shot him the finger.

He smiled and shot one back.

Suddenly the smell of mango tangerine returned and Tim appeared carrying two different sized scripts. He placed the thicker one in front of Cera and the thinner one in front of Bal.

"Why is her role bigger than mine?" asked Bal, looking at the difference.

"Genetics," said Cera

Tim covered his mouth with his hand and then chimed in, "Just remember that it is not the size of the role that matters, it's the intensity with which you play the part."

Cera smirked and said, "Sure it is."

Again, he found himself at a loss for words. He was speechless at the audacity of this person he had just met. He had never had this problem before and had no idea how to proceed. She was easily the most annoying person he had ever come across and he found himself looking forward to some relaxing time back on Earth. Hopefully he would never have to deal with her again.

Tim smiled, but said nothing.

Beside a nearby pillar, Elley watched Balthazar with keen interest.

Bal gently traced the raised, golden lettering of the title with his fingertips and then turned to the first page of *The Loser*.

THE LOSER

SPREAD OUT YOUR WEIGHT LIKE YOU ARE ON ICE, LATCH ON.

I don't know where that voice came from, but at this point it really doesn't matter! They say that your entire life is supposed to flash before your eyes when you are about to die.

So far I haven't seen shit.

I mean, come on! Am I asking too much for a few angels to appear and let me know that everything is going to be fine? I guess so! True, I haven't sustained a life ending injury, but I know that one is on the way and there is not a damn thing I can do to stop it.

At least the scenery surrounding me on the side of this cliff is nice. The rugged beauty of the Highlands here on the Isle of Skye is breathtaking. Literally. The sky is a deep azure blue and there are fluffy white clouds drifting along on the warm afternoon breeze. All around I see the purple heather sprouting from the almost vertical ground surrounding me.

Several hundred feet below there are some big, sharp looking rocks and several Hairy Cows.

Fucking cows.

I don't trust them.

It wouldn't surprise me if they helped to plan the entire set of circumstances that led me to this moment. They don't fool me. I know they are much more cunning than they let on, as they stare innocently up at me, eating their cud. I bet they have even called their cow-bookies to place a wager on which rock I'm going to land on.

I swear if I survive this, I am going to eat all the beef I can find.

You know, this is the story of me life. Here I am, hanging on to the side of a cliff like a giant squirrel, in imminent danger of falling to my death and all I can think about is getting even with some Hairy Cows.

I truly am a loser.

I have always tried to succeed, to win at anything; but it was never in the cards. As far back as I can remember, I have always failed miserably at everything I've tried. Everything.

The worst part is that I kept trying, thinking that someday my luck would turn around and I would finally win. I guess I was wrong. Damn.

I always had bad luck, even as a kid.

I was born in the second roughest section of an industrial town in the early 1970's. That should have been my first indication that something was wrong.

I remember those hideous, plaid bell bottoms that seemed to swallow my feet and get stuck in the chain of my bike. For those people who have never experienced the joy of riding quickly down the street, sitting on the banana seat of your bike and trying not to wipe out on the asphalt because your pant leg is caught in your chain, you haven't missed a lot! There were many times when my pants decided to work against me, and the numerous skinned knees were the result.

The local playground was not much better. I was bullied there a lot. See, I was very scrawny for my age with white blond hair and thick glasses.

I was an easy target.

Kids used to surround me in a circle and take turns pushing me back and forth. One time they even put fresh dog shit down my shirt and pressed it against my back. I told my dad and we went down to find them, but by that point everyone had vanished. Cowards.

Another time, I was getting a drink from the fountain and the local bully decided it would be funny to come up behind me and hit me on the back of the head. The blow caused my new, permanent teeth to smash into the metal water spout, chipping several of them.

It was always like that because I never fought back. I couldn't fight back. I wasn't big enough.

In primary school I was routinely chased home by groups of children who would take turns throwing rocks at me. I used to hide in the backyard of the neighbour and wait for them to leave so I wouldn't be hurt anymore. The neighbour would call my mom and she would come up the street to get me.

It was a rough couple of years.

Then one day my parents told me to start fighting back. They told me never to start a fight, but if there was no other choice, make sure to end it.

So I did.

I started swinging and didn't stop.

Then my dad received a promotion and we moved cities.

Our neighbourhood was nice and new, but my school was old and rough. Because I was the new kid, everyone decided to see how I would fit into the schoolyard pecking order.

By this time I had managed to gain weight so I wouldn't be so scrawny anymore, but that just added to the arsenal that the local kids would use against me. Instead of being made fun of because I was so skinny, now I was made fun of because I was fat.

I just wanted to be left alone, but nobody would allow that.

I became angry and let my fists do the negotiating with the local bullies. I fought so often that I was down in the principal's office at least three times per week and my parents were quickly becoming permanent fixtures at the school

I was labelled a trouble maker by the teachers and several of them went out of their way to make my life as difficult as possible. I tried to tell them that I never started the fights, but they wouldn't listen. I was always the one who was caught and punished, especially if the fight involved one of their favourite "pets".

I still remember one such pet named Josh. He would call me names, hit me in the back of the head and then run away to stand beside a teacher on yard duty because he knew that I couldn't do a thing about it. Eventually I caught him, only to have him gouge my cheek with his nails. I had blood dripping from four long gash marks on my face and I ended up getting a weeks worth of detention for it!

Then a few months later, Josh was calling me names again and then he hit me in the mouth with a hard chunk of dirt. He tried to run away, but I caught him and put him in a headlock. I was about to start beating him when he reached up and scratched my face - again! Then as if on cue, around the corner of the school came his favourite teacher. Do you think that he got in trouble? No! I was told to apologise to Josh! Can you believe that? The teacher was not interested in my side of the story and when I refused to apologise, I was sent back to the office.

This cycle continued for many years and I was even sent to anger counselling without my parents knowledge or consent.

To this day I do not understand what the point of it was. There was some lady who was trying to be sensitive and gain my trust so I would "open up to her". What she didn't realise was that there were no deep seeded issues why I was fighting so much. She asked me why I fought and

I told her; I doubt she believed me either.

What is it about the school system that makes it so easy for teachers to label children and so difficult for them to break out of that mould?

I must have been an enigma for them. I was a fighter, but also very good at schoolwork, especially English. I read everything I could find.

Books did not judge me or expect me to be anything I wasn't. At anytime I could crawl into my bedroom, open a book and instantly be taken someplace far away from my surroundings. I found comfort within their bindings, a spectator in someone else's dream.

I wonder is anyone will ever write about me? Who would believe the story? Especially now, with my fingers clenched into the loamy soil, high above a pack of Hairy Cows and several sheep.

I see. The cows must have sent out a message to the sheep to come an watch this silly human hanging onto the side of the cliff. The sheep probably are the collection agents for the cow-bookies and want to make certain that all bets are upheld. Damn sheep. If I survive this, I swear I'm going to eat as much mutton as I can!

Still, all things considered, they are fairly cute and women seem to love them.

Women.

Now there are creatures that I have no idea about. Seriously, the more I have learned about them, the more I realise that I know absolutely nothing! It has always been that way.

Ever since I was a kid, I was never good with members of the opposite sex. They seemed to be interested, but I lacked the ability to bring their interest to fruition.

For my first eighteen years of life, I only had mild success with women. I was able to hold their hand and if I was lucky, get a kiss on the cheek at the end of the night. This was extremely frustrating because all my friends were getting laid on a regular basis. I couldn't figure out what I was doing wrong, but then I discovered that the secret of attracting women came from inside. The key was confidence.

As I grew more confident with myself, women seemed to come out of the woodwork. Everyone seemed to believe that this meant more "horizontal dancing" for me, but that couldn't be further from the truth.

I learned that I had the innate ability to screw things up. It seemed as though Fate had decided I would forever be close to the finish line, but unable to cross.

Probably my most famous example would be with a woman named Karin whom I had the pleasure of meeting while I was an Exchange Student in Boras, Sweden. It was my senior year of High School and I thought that a change of scenery would be fun, so I signed up for a year living abroad.

My highschool in Sweden was segmented into different classes that studied different things, similar to the way a University in North America would work. My class had a total of forty people, six of which were male. It was as though the universe had decided to give me a break and surround me with the most beautiful women Sweden had to offer. It was my own personal slice of heaven, and Karin was the head angel.

You should have seen this woman, she was gorgeous.

To put this in perspective, I have never been tongue-tied around a woman before, and this lady made it impossible for me to speak. It wasn't just her long legs, hard body and beautiful face, but the very presence she seemed to convey when she entered the room. I couldn't keep my eyes off her, and it was obvious from her reaction that she was interested in more than my good looks.

This sounds simple, doesn't it? If only that were the case!

For some strange reason, we were never able to get together, something always happened to stop us.

For example, I was invited to her birthday party in early February at a bar in a nearby town. We did shots, funnelled beer and I took it as a good sign that she grabbed my crotch to distract me during an arm wrestling match with one of her friends.

Everything seemed to be going perfectly and I was about to make my move on the dancefloor when I got momentarily distracted by a pint of beer that one of my friends had bought me. When I turned back, another Swedish guy had slithered into my place and was making out with Karin in the corner of the room! I was not pleased, but the beer was good and the party was jumping, so I made the best of the situation.

Similar things happened to me all year long. Everytime I turned my back on a woman, another slimy guy would slither up and take my spot. I would have punched them in the head, but when you are acting as an ambassador of your country, you have to think of the image you want to portray.

There were many times during the year when Karin and I almost hooked up, but it never materialised. Then, at the end of the school year, the entire student body got together on a nearby beach for a giant party called "Almansdagen". It was an all day thing and many people had brought their tents to spend the night.

I grabbed several cans of beer and headed down to the party in the early evening. I remember talking to someone and from out of nowhere, Karin came bouncing up and gave me a giant hug.

I took this as a good sign.

She asked me if I was interested in a beer drinking contest where the loser had to go skinny dipping in the lake.

Yes, a very good sign.

Of course I agreed and I can honestly tell you that I have never finished a beer so quickly in my entire life! Karin took only a few sips from her can and said, "Oh, it seems I lose."

As good as her word, Karin immediately went down to the lake, stripped naked and jumped in. What can I say? She looked even better naked than I could imagine. She asked me if I wanted to join her, but for some reason I declined and said that the water was too cold.

A few hours, and many beers later, Karin reappeared and we started talking. The conversation (which I have replayed in my mind over and over again) went something like this.

"I see you have one can of beer left," said Karin.

"Yes. Why?" I replied suspiciously.

"Well, I'm all out, so I will make you a deal. If you give me your last can of beer, I will give you a blowjob right now in the woods."

I wanted to make sure I heard her correctly, so I said, "Let me get this straight. If I give you my last can of beer, you will give me a blowjob right now?"

Karin smiled mischievously and said, "Exactly. What do you think?"

It was a dream come true. I wanted to say yes, but instead I heard myself say, "Under normal circumstances I would say yes, but this is my last beer."

What was I thinking? Looking back now, I should have given her the beer, but at that point in time, I really liked my beer.

One would think that would be enough to finish me off, but it would appear that Fate had other plans for me that night.

Several hours later, thanks to another classmate who had lost patience with the both of us not getting together, I finally got the opportunity to kiss Karin.

It was amazing.

Now, I will let you in on a secret about Scandinavian women that nobody will tell you. When they get turned on, watch out because there is no turning them off. I thought the urban legends about Swedish women were false - I was wrong.

After half and hour of making out with Karin, she literally dragged me back to a giant army tent that the class had for the night. It was pitch black, but I could hear the voices of my classmates coming from inside its interior. I suggested we should move to the woods because of the people in the tent, but Karin said that she didn't care.

After a brief moment of consideration, I dove headlong into the tent.

Just as I reached out to close the tent flap, I heard a familiar voice from about ten feet away. It was Camellia, one of my friends from school. She asked me if I still needed a ride home because she was leaving. I said no and that I had decided to stay the night. Camellia then told me that if I didn't go home, my host family would be very disappointed with me. Talk about a knife in the heart!

I ducked my head into the tent and found myself locked in Karin's warm embrace. How I wanted to stay, but I couldn't. I told her I had to leave and the reason why.

She wasn't happy.

I got a ride back to my house with Camellia, only to discover the next day that my host family was surprised that I came home. They had been expecting me to spend the night.

One would think that as I grew older, my luck would improve. It would have to, right? But, to tell you the truth, it seemed to maintain the same direction; straight down! After the notorious beer incident with Karin, I slowed down my beveraging to the point where it was non-existent, just in case the offer of sex ever came up again. For years, my virtual sobriety refused to pan out and no offers whatsoever found their way to me.

That all changed earlier this year when I moved to Liverpool for my third year of University as an exchange student. All signs pointed to an incredible year of sin; the co-ed dorm, my newly rescuplted body and of course, my accent.

Things started with a bang, literally. Within sixteen hours of setting down in this country, I had already been attacked by a beautiful, blond haired, blue eyed woman who went by the nickname of Loo. I resisted, of course, but I looked on it as my responsibility to further foreign relations.

Then the beer began.

Between the middle of September and the beginning of December, I must have consumed around three hundred pints of beer in and around the Student Union Hall on campus. Yep, my mistake.

It all began with a woman named Dawn who always seemed to appear late in the evening after we had a "few" pints. I say we, because my mate who went by the nickname of Muddy was usually by my side.

Muddy was an international student from Africa who had an obsession with video games and Brandon Lee. He had a great sense of humour and was the first person to make me feel welcome in the dorm. I still remember sitting down at a table by myself for dinner when he slid himself into a chair across from me and didn't say a word, just stared.

I introduced myself and he said to call him Muddy because it was much easier than trying to pronounce his name. I didn't know what to think, but he said that we could be friends and I should come join the rest of the residence at a nearby table. The rest, as they say, is history.

Muddy was never at a shortage for female company. I thought it could have something to do with his dreadlocks, but he insisted that it was merely a "black thing".

Sure it was.

Whatever his secret, Dawn seemed to pay particular attention to both of us and I remember discussing which one of us would get her first. I believed it was me and Muddy insisted it was him. This continued for several months, and then in January we saw her in the daylight when both of us were sober.

All I can say is that darkness and alcohol were this ladies friends.

I turned to Muddy and told him that he was clearly the correct choice for her and I would honourably bow out of the contest. Muddy responded by insisting that Dawn and I were meant to be together and he would definitely not stand in our way. It was very kind of him to make the offer, but in the end we took off running and ended up playing a fighting game on his computer.

Next, there was Paula, a drop-dead gorgeous brunette whom I had lived with the previous year and who decided to come to the United Kingdom for a mini vacation. It was her last year of school and she wanted to it to "go out with a bang."

I was pleased to hear from her and offered her a place to stay for a few days while she was exploring the countryside. The year had been kind to her and she was in the best shape of her life. Her boobs looked firm enough to crush cans of beer with them and her ass! All I could say is, wow.

We hung out for the evening and drank like there was no tomorrow. I was having an excellent time when she asked if I still gave massages because she was sore after doing so much travelling and my hands "were just what she needed."

I didn't think anything of it and immediately offered to give her one after we were finished our drinks. I was impressed by how quickly she finished her beer and before I knew it, we were back in my dorm room and she was laying face down on my bed. I straddled her and started rubbing her back for her when she asked if I had any massage oil left.

I said yes, but won't that ruin your top? She replied that was a good point and proceeded to take her top off and throw it across the room while I got the oil from my closet. I turned around to find her bra on the ground beside the bed and when I commented about it, she told me that just like her shirt, she didn't want anything to get on her bra.

That seemed logical, so I straddled her and gave her an excellent massage. After around half an hour, I began to think that maybe she might be interested in me, so I leaned down near her face and waited for her to make the first move.

Nothing happened.

So I continued chatting with her until suddenly she sighed loudly, grabbed her bra and said that she had to go and sleep because she had a long trip ahead of her. I smiled, said I understood and gave her a hug goodnight.

She left the next morning before I could say goodbye and I have not heard from her since.

I think I might have missed something there.

Also during this same two and a half month block of beveraging, I had the opportunity to fulfil every mans dream; almost.

On my way out of the pub one night, I was stopped at the door by two beautiful women. One told me that her friend liked me, then the other one said that her friend also like me. I gave my head a shake to ensure that I heard them correctly, and they told me that I should come by their house sometime soon. Of course I agreed right away and they told me their address. I assured them I would stop by, but by the time I got outside, I had forgotten not only their address, but what they looked like! I wanted to kick my own ass! It just wasn't fair!

I didn't see them for months after, and believe me, I checked! Then a few weeks ago, while I was emptying the bar of all the alcho-pops they had because they were on sale, I looked up and from out of the crowd of dancing students, both women emerged and headed directly towards me.

Each woman kissed one of my cheeks, then grabbed by hand and led me onto the dance floor. I couldn't believe my good fortune! After all, this was the kind of thing that I had only read about in various men's magazines! I dirty danced with both of them, one on each thigh, and they took turns licking my fillings!

It was amazing.

They asked me what I was doing after the bar, and I told them I wasn't sure. They said good because I was "coming back to theirs".

By this point of the night, I had to take a leak so badly that I was ready to burst. So I excused myself and set a new overland speed record heading to the nearest bathroom.

What I didn't know was that it was the last song of the night and by the time I got back, all the lights were on and the two women were no where to be found! I searched high and low, but they were gone.

If only I had known that it was the last song of the night, I would have waited until I had gone back to their house! I could lie and say that I am not bitter, but yes, yes I am!

You know, I'm not certain why the Fates enjoyed tormenting me so much. Perhaps it was because they knew that I could handle anything they threw my way, or it was because they were just jerks. Either way, I'm not sure what to think!

Then there was the time just before I came to this continent when I had perhaps the roughest three weeks of my entire life.

It started when I was driving up to my girlfriends house for a wedding of one of my friends. I was about half an hour away when I noticed that my engine was making a strange sound, sort of a whirring noise. Now I am not a mechanic; in fact, the only thing I know about cars is that you put gas in them and they go. But even I knew that a sound like that was not good and would probably be expensive.

Shortly thereafter, fifth gear ceased to exist.

I said, "Oh no! That's not good! No fifth gear! Please let there be a fourth!"

I downshifted and fourth gear kicked in - barely. Then about fifteen minutes later, I started hearing the same sound as before. Luckily I made it to the outskirts of her city before I was forced to drop to third gear.

The next day I dropped it off at her families' mechanic with a disturbing sensation that the damage was going to be expensive.

I was right.

I received a call later that day and it turned out that the transmission was destroyed and could not be repaired; it need to be replaced and the part would not be available until after the weekend. Normally this would not have been a problem, but I was supposed to start a new job at seven a.m. on the following Monday morning, a mere three days away. So I told the guy to please fix the car and to install a used transmission if at all possible.

Then I called my work.

It wasn't pleasant.

I managed to track down the Human Resources lady and inform her that I would be unable to start work on Monday because of car troubles. Then I asked her if were at all possible to start on Tuesday and stay late to make up for anything I had missed the previous day. I even offered to show her a copy of the receipt on Tuesday to prove that I was not lying about the car problems.

She informed me that when they hire people to start on a Monday, they are expected to start on the Monday, not Tuesday, and the people that do not show up on the Monday were not invited back for the Tuesday.

What a nice lady.

So I got fired from a job that I hadn't even started yet.

The next day at the wedding reception, my girlfriend did this amazing athletic manoeuvre and caught the bouquet. She actually looked like one of those flying squirrels that jump from tree to tree over long distances. Her feet left the ground and she dove forward to snatch the flowers out of mid air. If she were an owl and the bouquet were a mouse, it would be all over for the rodent in a heart beat!

According to one of my friends that I was sitting with, when she caught the flowers my face contorted in horror and I screamed, "Oh shit!"

Now I do not remember saying anything like that, but then again, I did have a few carbonated beverages by that point in the night, so anything was possible.

The next day I was hungover and while the girlfriend was out shopping with her parents, her little brother, or Love Monkey as I call him, wanted to play some catch with me. So I figured, what the heck?

We went outside, through the swarms of mosquitoes that looked at me like an all you can eat buffet, and positioned ourselves on the road. I had managed to find a glove that was at least two sizes too small for me, but I did not see the potential harm in using it.

My mistake.

Love Monkey threw the first pitch to me and I just misplayed the ball. It hit the palm of my hand, bounced off, hit my upper forearm and ricocheted right into my face! I had lace marks etched into my cheek and a black eye to match my pounding head.

Love Monkey was so worried that I would be upset and do something evil to get back at him.

He was right.

Later that day when he was walking by me to go into the laundry room, I swung a bag of ice around and hit him in the nuts with it.

I felt a bit better.

The next day, Monday, I found out that my car would not be ready until the following day because of difficulty finding the used transmission.

So I finally get my car on the Tuesday and take off out of that city like a bat out of hell, wearing one of my new muscle shirts with the windows in the car rolled down because my little beast did not have air conditioning. This was late summer, so it was very hot and I had my left arm hanging out the window.

My mistake again.

By the time I got home, the left side of my body was scarlet and I resembled a freshly cooked lobster.

The discomfort was great, but not as great as when I blew out my "o" ring two days later and decided to go see a doctor to make sure nothing was wrong.

I went to a local walk in clinic because I did not have a family doctor any more, mine had retired. The door listed five doctors on call that day, four men and one woman. I thought my odds of getting a male doctor were pretty good.

Obviously not good enough.

Into the examining room walked this old, decrepit woman that had the dead eyes of a goldfish and a face like she had been sucking on lemons. I told her what the problem was and she told me to strip and hop on the examing table. Normally I rather enjoyed being naked, but with sub-zero air conditioned wasteland of an office, I was certain there would not be much of a show.

The next thing I know, my butt cheeks are pried apart like an oyster shell and I hear this dead voice tell me that she was going to insert a scope.

Insert?

Before I could finish my thought, I felt something hollow and huge force its way inside me. It was a pressure unlike anything I had ever experienced before and all I could think was try not to clench, relax.

Easier said than done.

I thought the swirling motion was a nice touch.

Then she removed the object so quickly that my sphincter slammed shut like a bear trap. My head was still swimming from the new sensations when I heard her say that she was going to insert a finger.

A finger? Please God, let her have small hands!

Then she jammed what I could only assume was her fist, into my ass and moved it around in much the same way as you would to remove the last vestiges of peanut butter from the corner of the jar. From a distance I heard her say that there appears to be some swelling.

You think?

So after being worn as a glove, I walked out of that office like I had just been horseback riding for a month and headed to the local pharmacy for a rubber ring and some pain killers.

By this time it was getting dark and I turned on my headlight so I could see. I say headlight because only one was working. The other was experiencing an electrical problem that caused the running lights and high beams to work, but the regular headlight refused to come on.

I was thinking about how my luck had been going when a police cruiser passed me, slowed down, pulled behind me and turned on its lights. I immediately pulled into the gas station beside me, rolled down my window and turned off the car in an attempt to look co-operative and non-threatening. Normally I put the car into reverse, pull up the emergency brake and turn off the car. This time I was in such a hurry to appear friendly that I forgot to pull up the brake and put the car into reverse.

I left it in neutral.

Just as the cops got out of their car, my little beast started to roll backward; directly into their cruiser.

The thud of my car hitting theirs caused my stomach to drop and all

I could think was I'm going to prison. Oh well, at least I would not be a stranger to rectal exams.

The police officers were not happy.

Luckily there was no damage to the cruiser and I received two one-hundred and ten dollar tickets for my trouble. One for the broken headlight and the other for failing to change over my license to my current address.

It was a rough seven day stretch.

Heck, it had been a rough life.

And now here I am, holding onto the soft side of a cliff, reminiscing about what might have been.

Damn, I really am a loser.

The sky had turned a deep crimson, setting the Highlands ablaze with colour. It was a beautiful sunset. If only I had a camera.

Wait! I do have a camera, right here, looped through my belt. If I can just bring my one hand down slightly, I can open the pouch and have a funny photo to show everyone back home. Gently.

Suddenly the piece of earth I had been holding onto gave way without warning and I felt myself falling backward.

This was going to hurt.

ACT FOUR

He was right.

The rugged beauty of the highlands surged past him like a river of green and he slammed into the jagged rocks at the bottom of the ancient mountain in much the same way as an egg would on concrete.

There was a momentary surge of pain and then it was gone, replaced by a deep warmth that radiated through his shattered body. He was screwed and he knew there was nothing that could be done for him.

He still blamed the hairy coos.

The early evening sky was aglow with rich layers of colour and the first cool breeze of night caressed his face like the gentle breath of mother earth. He tried to blink, but found that he could not take his eyes from the endless warmth offered by the skies.

If this was what dying was like, he was happy that would be his final sight.

As if on cue, the silhouetted heads of two hairy cows suddenly appeared in his line of sight and seemed to stare in amusement at his situation. They absent-mindedly chewed their cud and he could imagine they were taking bets on how much longer he had to live. In fact, he could swear he could hear them talking.

"Where were you?" asked the first cow in a strangely familiar voice, "It's supposed to be your job to look after him, not strut around like you own the place!"

"Well, excuse me," replied the other cow. "Let's see how well you do with hair in your eyes! He's lucky I even saw enough to warn him to spread his body weight out and latch onto the side of the cliff like he was on ice."

The first cow rolled its bulging eyes and snorted, "Do you see any ice? You know we are in Scotland, right? I mean, seriously! Ice? What were you thinking?"

"Well, I don't see you doing anything about it!"

Talking cows?

"Yes, Balthy," replied the first cow, "Marky here was supposed to be your guardian angel and make sure that nothing happened to you. But it's obvious that some people, who will remain nameless, cannot seem to say no to anything."

"Just like you and doughnuts," replied Marky. "Do you think that I am blind, Tim? Don't think that I haven't noticed the passion crème ones have gone missing from the cafe and found their way to your thighs."

"Oh!" shrieked Tim, "I can't believe that you just went there! I'm so flustered right now that I need a nice pomtini to help calm me down. This discussion is far from over! Just wait till we get home!"

It must be the concussion from the fall.

"Yes, that was definitely part of it," said Marky, "But your body is also dying. The lease on this rental is almost up and you are being booted out. Usually things run a lot smoother when *everyone* does their job."

Tim snorted, licked his nose and said nothing.

He was dying and his last thoughts were to be of talking cows. Yep, the hits just kept on coming. He truly was a loser.

"Don't say that about yourself," said Tim, casting Marky a dirty look, "Believe it or not, we are Angels and are here to take you somewhere very special."

"Heaven?" he whispered.

"Exactly," replied Marky.

"So I made it after all. I'm surprised."

"Why?" asked Tim, turning his head to the side.

"I've done so many bad things in my life; so many mistakes, so many missed opportunities."

"Like the women?" asked Marky, "Don't worry. We know about everything."

He felt his face burn with embarrassment.

"In fact," continued Tim, "There were many times when we walked alongside you and experienced life as you lived it."

The sunset grew brighter.

"We laughed when you laughed and cried when you cried. You played your part well and even though you made mistakes, it is the sum of your life experiences that are truly important. You had an amazing life, and now it is time to come home for a rest."

Perhaps he wasn't such a loser after all.

"Are you ready?" asked Tim.

He felt himself smile.

The sky grew brighter and he felt the soft, translucent warmth of the crimson light envelope him in its embrace. It gently drew him upward into itself, into pure beauty and he felt a shiver of excitement similar to the wait on Christmas Eve when he was a child, knowing that a magnificent present was awaiting him in the morning.

The excitement, like the speed at which he was travelling, increased exponentially with each passing second. In the distance he could make out a patch of light unlike anything he had ever seen before. Its size was both enormous and tiny at the same time and it seemed to dance and swirl with a mirad of colours; many of which he had never seen before. It pulsated and twinkled like a living being and he swore that he could hear music and singing.

It sounded like there was one heck of a party going on and for the first time in his life, he felt as though he was welcome.

The light grew brighter and brighter until it obscured everything else and then faded away as quickly as it came. He found himself standing in front of a beautifully carved, wooden gate, staring at row upon row of overstuffed chairs and tables.

He was confused.

"You look confused, Balthy," said a voice that he recognised as Tim, the talking cow.

He followed the sound of the voice and discovered that it came from a person that was sitting at a table near the entrance of the cafe that had short, black, spiky hair with frosted tips, sideburns and a neatly trimmed goatee. The person was immaculately dressed in a silky, salmon coloured dress shirt, white khakis, and a tan belt that perfectly matched his sandals. But the most interesting thing was the pair of fluffy, white wings that jutted out of his back, right by the shoulder blades.

He was staring at an angel.

A real angel.

"Of course I am a real angel," said Tim as he uncrossed his legs, stood up and walked toward him, "Did you think I was joking back on earth?"

He was so stunned that all he could do was shrug his shoulders and think to himself, where were the enormous, pearly gates?

Tim walked behind him, gently reached out with a perfectly manicured hand and placed it on his shoulder. The strength of his grasp caught him off guard and Tim said, "Now don't worry. The pearly gates do exist, but they are just getting a much needed facelift. After millennia of souls going back and forth, something needed to be done. So when the casting director sent out a general memo asking for suggestions on what to do, I immediately suggested painting it a shimmering, iridescent candy colour. That way it will match whatever light is on it at the time. It would be perfect for parties."

Colour changing gates? Mind reading angels? A cafe where there should be clouds? He wasn't sure what to say. But where was St. Peter with the book of his life? Surely he had to be here.

Tim gave his shoulder a gentle squeeze and said, "Oh, Petey is around somewhere, and no doubt up to something. He has a habit of showing up for a guest appearance in people's stories, so if you meet him, don't be fooled by his saintly appearance. He has a wicked sense of humour and loves to play practical jokes on people. He even got me once, but I have something special in mind for him. Oh, and we don't use books anymore; we've switched to electronic PDA's. It's much faster and you can stay in contact with everyone."

"What's a PDA?"

"Oh, they're not on Earth yet. But they will be shortly."

Suddenly he heard the sound of heavy metal music and Tim said, "Excuse me for a minute," and placed a finger to his ear. "Hello? Yes, this is he, fabulous and in person! How can I help you? Really? Yes, Balthy is right here. You want to do what? Now? But he just got back. Yes, I can do that. Absolutely! See you in five. Chow."

Tim tapped his ear and then turned excitedly toward him and said, "You will never guess who that was! It seems that you have caught the eye of the casting director himself and he likes your work so much that he is sending his son, the assistant casting director, by to meet with you about another role!"

"What do you mean by 'another role'? And why do you keep calling me Balthy?"

Tim's eyes grew large and he covered his mouth with hand and gasped, "That's right! I'm so sorry, Balthy. I was so excited that I forgot. Of course you don't know what I am talking about, you just got back. Honestly, I am so scatterbrained at times that I am certain I would forget my wings if they were not attached. Here, come with me."

Tim quickly led him to the table where he had just been sitting and motioned for him to sit in one of the overstuffed chairs. He didn't know why, but he could swear that he had been there before.

"You have been," said Tim, sitting down across from him. "In fact, you have been here three times before, and each time we have this exact conversation over a delicious coffee beverage and a piece of my succulent quiche."

"You make quiche?" he asked excitedly.

"Of course I do! Would you like a piece?"

He nodded his head and when he looked at the table, a thick wedge of fluffy quiche and a huge cup of steaming latte had appeared in front of him.

"Now go on and eat up," said Tim, "He will be here soon and I want you to make a good impression because I think he has something special in mind for you."

He wasn't sure what Tim was talking about, but all things considered, it seemed to fit perfectly with the strange day he had been having. If he was in a coma, he hoped that he could remember all of this because it would make one heck of a story. He picked up the fork and was amazed at how easily it slipped into the golden pie.

Tim said nothing and leaned forward expectantly as the quiche touched his lips. It was delicious and unlike anything he had ever experienced in his life. As he chewed, flavours burst along his tongue and filled his entire being with joy and memories.

Everything came back to him. His previous lives as a whore, a professor and a loser were as fresh in his memory as the taste of the quiche was on his palate.

He blinked quickly and focused his eyes on Tim, seeing him once again for the first time. He smiled and said, "Hello Tim. You are looking good! I like the frosted tips look and for the record, I don't know what Mark was talking about. Nothing has gone to your thighs."

Tim blushed and replied, "Oh Balthy! Stop! I just thought I would try something different. Do you really like it?"

"I do, and that colour looks amazing on you. It really brings out the rose in your cheeks."

"Why thank you. It's nice to know that someone notices," said Tim in a loud enough voice for their entire section to hear it.

Balthazar wasn't certain, but he could almost swear that he saw an angel at a nearby table roll his eyes and then continue his conversation with a lady that sat across from him.

She looked familiar.

Very familiar.

Their eyes met.

It was Cera.

Bal felt his insides cringe at the sight of her and suddenly had to resist hitting her with his chair.

"Now behave," said Tim with a strange smile playing at the corner of his mouth. "I know that the two of you get along as well as plaid and stripes, but sometimes the most unexpected things can happen. After all, who's to say that you would not work together in a future story?"

"I say," replied Bal as he shot Cera a dirty look which was quickly returned in kind, "I would rather tongue kisses a hair cow than work with that."

He motioned with his hand toward Mark and Cera's table, when he noticed out of the corner of his eye that she had motioned back with only a single digit.

Bal's jaw hung slack in amazement at the crude gesture aimed at him and Tim covered his mouth to try and stifle the laughter bubbling up inside. He leaned forward and with great difficulty managed to say, "I think you've met your match, Balthy. She is quite a handful and her reviews all say that she is a very accomplished actress."

"Sure she is," muttered Bal under his breath, "Accomplished at being a pain in my ass."

"More than you know," said Tim.

He had a bad feeling about this.

"What do you mean?"

"Do you remember that intimate run in you had with the doctor?"

Tim started to laugh.

Oh no. It couldn't be.

He face was burning as he looked over and saw Cera smirk, stick out her arm and do a swirling motion with her fist.

He didn't know what to say, so he just stuck out his bottom lip and nodded to himself.

Of course it had to be her.

Tim doubled over in laughter and had tears streaming down his face. He was gasping for air and made high pitched, squeaking noises as he tried to regain a measure of composure.

"I'm...so...sorry...Balthy," said Tim as he wiped the tears away from his eyes, "I know I shouldn't laugh at your situation, but it was so funny when we saw it the first time, and now to see your reaction in person is priceless!"

"I'm glad my discomfort brought you pleasure," replied Bal, licking his lips and raising his left eyebrow. "It's good to know that I am so highly thought of, that I get to experience such unique sensations in my roles."

From the nearby table, Cera chimed in, "Unique sensation? I saw that smile on your face!"

He was speechless.

"And didn't you just fall of a cliff? How did you manage that?"

Balthazar shrugged meekly and said quietly, "I was running and kind of fell."

Cera smiled and shook her head in disbelief, "Let me get this straight. You decided to run along a narrow dirt path, cut into the side of a nearly vertical hill, hundreds of feet in the air?"

He squirmed uncomfortably and replied, "Yes. But it wasn't my fault! It was the influence of those people I was with."

"Uh huh. Did you not notice the signs posted everywhere that said not to run?"

"Well, yeah, but..."

"So you decided to ignore the warnings and followed the lead of two guys that ended up leaving you to fall to your death?"

"But it was kind of funny."

Cera tilted her head to the side and said, "It seems like what we consider as funny is completely different from one another."

Balthazar turned away and mumbled, "At least I have a sense of humour."

"What was that?" snapped Cera, her upper body moving forward aggressively in her chair.

Balthazar stopped, clenched his fists and turned toward Cera. "I said, unlike you, you cold-hearted, calculating, know-it-all pain in the ass, I have a sense of humour!"

Cera's eyes narrowed and she opened her mouth to say something, but before she could, Balthazar continued, "Shut it! I've had enough of people like you who feel the need to always point out and then comment on another person's faults! I've dealt with them over several lives and that is quite enough! I'm not spending my afterlife dealing with the likes of you!"

"Fine," snorted Cera as she whipped around in her chair and focused her attention on Marky.

"Good." snarled Balthazar as he turned to focus his attention on Tim.

Tim and Marky exchanged knowing glances and did their best not to smirk.

"You must be Balthazar," said a deep voice behind him.

Tim had stopped smiling and was absent mindedly straightening his shirt. In fact, the entire cafe had gone strangely silent and there was a strange electricity in the air as he turned around to see what all the fuss was about.

Standing directly behind him was a man of average build in his mid-thirties, dressed in a flowing white suit and collared shirt. He was tanned with a beard and had long, dirty-blond hair that was tied back in a pony tail.

Two things struck Bal as odd about this man. One was that he was wearing sandals with a suit and the other was that in spite of staring directly at him, he could not give an accurate description of what the man looked like.

Strange.

"Do you mind if I join you?" asked the man.

"Please do," replied Bal, motioning for him to pull up a chair.

The man unbuttoned his suit jacket and flopped down into the overstuffed chair. When he was comfortable, he extended his hand toward Bal and said, "Hello Balthazar, my name is Josephsson, J. Josephsson, and I am the assistant casting director for the entire site."

"It's a pleasure to meet you," replied Bal, extending his own hand and grasping the hand of the assistant casting director. His hand was thick, strong and callused; the hand of a tradesman, though how an assistant casting director had such features was beyond him. They shook and then Bal said, "And this is Tim. The Angel of Death, Greetings and he makes an excellent quiche."

The man smiled warmly and said, "I know Tim quite well. He used to do security for us, but now he has really come into his own with his current position. If you ever get the chance, you should go to one of his parties, they are amazing. By the way Tim, I like what you have done with your hair."

Tim blushed, but remained silent.

"What can I do for you?" asked Bal, still trying to focus on the man's features.

"To be honest," began Josephsson, "I would like you to consider a role that has been written especially for you. Normally these types of roles go to more experienced actors, but we have been keeping a close eye on you for quite some time and we believe that you are the perfect person for it."

"Really?" asked Bal. He was shocked that he would be offered something like this, especially after only three roles.

"Yes," replied the man, "We know that you've had only had three roles, but each had different challenges that led you to this point. I know it is a lot to ask, but I would really appreciate it if you were to give it a try."

Bal nodded in agreement and quickly shot Cera a smug look.

"Sure," said Bal, "I would love to take a look at it. Do you have it with you?"

Josephsson nodded, but before he could place the thick manuscript in front of him, there was the strange sound of snakes slithering, followed by an overpowering smell of cheap aftershave and then someone was standing in front of them, flanked on either side by two of the largest, meanest looking men he had ever seen. The figure was dressed entirely in tailor made, red silk suit, with an ebony tie and the shiny leather shoes. He was clean shaven and had long, blond curls fall in waves onto his shoulders. But just like Josephsson, Bal could not focus on the features of the person.

Tim leapt to his feet and was about to tackle the figure when Josephsson motioned for him to stay put.

The figure in red smiled warmly at Tim and said, "Why, hello Tim. It's good to see you again. I trust the wounds have healed since our last meeting?"

Bal actually saw Tim's body begin to shake with pure rage, but he had to give him credit because he did not move. He continued to glare at the figures and the two bodyguards shifted uncomfortably under Tim's steely stare.

Josephsson smiled dismissively and said, "And what brings you by the Cafe, Lou? May I offer you a coffee or perhaps a nice slice of pie?"

Lou didn't miss a beat and replied, "No thanks, I do not have enough time. There is so much to do and so little time. You know what it's like."

Josephsson nodded and Lou continued, "I just thought I would drop by and check out the newest rising star in your label. I hear that he has already made quite the name for himself with a few challenging roles."

"That is very true. He has surprised us all, which is why we offer him such challenging roles. Balthazar, this is..."

"Cypher. Lou Cypher," blatantly interrupted Lou as he moved forward and extended a ring encrusted hand toward Balthazar.

Bal grasped Lou's hand and was amazed at how callused they were. It was the hand of someone who was no stranger to hard work; it was the hand of a warrior.

"It's a pleasure to meet you," said Bal.

"Yes, it could be," replied Lou as he stared intently at Balthazar.

The man's eyes bored a hole right through him and Bal felt as though he had no secrets from him.

"Lou here, is the head of our rival studio and he is always looking for new talent to represent," said Josephsson as he watched the interaction between Lou and Bal with great interest.

"There are two different studios?" asked Bal.

"Not really that different," said Lou, never taking his eyes off Bal, "We used to be part of the same studio, but there came a time when there was a slight difference of opinion about how to run things and we decided to split."

"You mean you were thrown out," muttered Tim with slight snarl in his voice.

Lou rolled his eyes dismissively and continued, "Thrown out, decided to split, fell, they are all semantics. The point is that there are other options for actors to consider. They don't have to be locked into the same studio, dealing with the same people over and over again, never having the ability to choose their roles. That's why I left..."

"Helped to leave."

"Whatever. Tim, you are just not fun anymore. Anyway, time to go and make some new deals, sign some new talent. I look forward to meeting you again, Bal. Here, take my card," said Lou as he reached into the inside pocket of his three piece suit and removed a business card.

Bal took the card and glanced down at it. The card was blood red with black writing on it that said, MR. LOU CYPHER, CEO, INFERNO PRODUCTIONS.

"If you would like to talk sometime, give me a call and we will do lunch. Until then, have a wonderful day! Bal, Tim, Josephsson." He nodded to each in turn and then vanished along with his bodyguards with the same sound of slithering snakes, but the overpowering smell of cheap aftershave remained, hanging in the air like a cloud of perpetual putrid ness.

Tim took a deep breath, stretched his neck and then sat back down in his chair and crossed his legs.

"I'm sorry about that Balthazar," said Josephsson, "Lou does not have a lot of social skills. Now where were we?"

"You were going to let me look at the next role which was specially written for me," said Balthazar, placing the card down on the table.

Josephsson nodded and placed a thick manuscript on the table in front of him. It was loosely bound with golden thread and written in raised, guilded lettering was the title of the story, *The Writer*.

Bal gently traced his fingers over the words and turned the page.

THE WRITER

His bottom lip flicked in and out subconsciously as he sat hunched on the uncomfortable blue couch. The electronic noise of the television did not help take his mind off his recent life-changing news.

He still felt numb. Even a full twenty-four hours later, it seemed like a horrible dream. His mind felt heavy, weary from too much thinking and far too little sleep. The bottom of his eyelids hurt and his eyes felt dry. It seemed like a giant piece of his chest was missing, replaced with emptiness and a dull pain, reminiscent of a giant chasm of suffering.

Even after trying to figure things out, he still didn't understand why she decided that she needed a break from him. Was it another man? Possible, but quite unlikely. Another woman? That would make things easier to take, but that wasn't it, he was sure.

He knew that they were in trouble and had been for some time, but he never thought she would be so cold, callous and calculated about it. He could still remember the conversation. It was as fresh in his mind as the wounds were deep.

"Hello?" he said, answering the phone and placing his salmon and rice dinner on the arm of the couch.

"Hello," came the voice of his girlfriend on the other end of the phone. She sounded different, distant and cold.

"It is good to hear from you, Gerri," he said, quickly swallowing the last vestiges of food in his mouth so he would not chew in her ear.

There was a brief silence, and then she said, "You may not think so after this conversation."

He knew what was coming.

"I've been doing a lot of soul searching over the last few days and I've come to a conclusion."

Uh-oh.

"Yes?"

She paused for breath, it seemed like forever, and then the tirade came.

"I don't know if it is you or me, but I've decided that we need to take a break from each other."

There wasn't a physical blow, but he could swear that a giant foot had just crashed into his stomach. He felt as though he were falling into an abyss from which only darkness and pain emanated.

Still, he managed to keep his voice from shaking and after a few seconds replied, "What do you mean, take a break?"

She didn't miss a beat.

"I mean we should have absolutely no contact with each other from this point on, and if the feelings are true, then we can take it from there."

Emptiness. He felt emptiness envelope him.

"Fair enough," he said as he waited for this nightmare to end and to wake up in his own bed. "But let me ask you one thing."

"And what's that?" she questioned curtly.

He took a deep breath, "Do you still love me?"

There was a momentary silence on the other end of the phone and she replied, "I don't know."

There it was: the knockout blow. Four years and nine months worth of commitment shattered by three simple words.

He felt the edges of his world begin to unravel.

The abyss welcomed him with open arms.

"Hmmm," he said, shocked by the lack of emotion exhibited by someone he loved with his entire being, "Have a good life."

Before she could say anymore, he took the portable phone away from his ear and hung up. It was the loudest silence he had ever heard.

He just sat there, staring at the television, hunger forgotten and all thoughts numb. How could someone do that? It was obvious that she had it planned for a long time, but how?

How could one person be so very wrong about another? He knew from the moment he first met her at their mutual friends stag and doe party that she was the one he had been searching for all his life.

She was the one.

For the first time in his existence, he had met someone that he could actually think about having more than just a one night fling with. He looked at her and saw their unborn children in her deep brown eyes. Physically, she was not his "type", but there was something special about her.

He had been scared of commitment and never let a single person, other than his immediate family, through the defences surrounding his heart. But over time she gradually broke through everyone of them until she was closer than anyone had ever been. It had taken over three years for him to trust her completely and now he wished it had never happened.

He should have kept her at a distance. If he had, the pain would not be as bad as it was now. He could have simply walked away and not thought about her ever again. If only it were that easy.

His stomach and throat were on fire. It felt like a giant hand was squeezing acid from his stomach into his oesophagus. He had always had acid reflux, but this time the burn was so intense that no medication could help him. With each burp, more of the lining of his throat burned away, and still he sat like a statue on the horrible, blue couch.

How could she say that she did not know if she loved him? It was a simple answer, yes or no.

He felt cold; not physically, but emotionally. It was as though someone came along and ripped all of the comfort away from his inside.

He thought he probably should cry, but couldn't. Crying was supposed to make you feel better, a way of cleansing your insides if you will. But he just couldn't do it. There was something profoundly unmasculine about crying, but what does that say about keeping your emotions locked so tightly inside that they cause a heart attack?

He wanted to hurt her. Not physically, but emotionally. He wanted her to suffer the kind of torment that wracked him to the core. The rage that he had kept in check for so many years had burst free of its prison and wanted retribution.

All he had to do was pick up the phone and call her. She would be at work and he could leave a message on the phone that told her exactly what he thought of her break and where she could jam it. Furthermore, he had thought of the ultimate thing to say to her; something that would slice her to the very core and shatter her emotionally for years to come. He would say that he finally understood why her ex-boyfriend cheated on her.

It would have the desired affect; he was certain of it. The rage fantasised about the tears that would stream down her face and the emotion-snapping self doubt that would race inside her. The pain would be exquisite and it would laugh as she curled into a foetal position from the sickness that overwhelmed her. It would gloat at her suffering and smile smugly as she threw up all night long. It wanted sorrow and to make her pay for everything that she had done to him.

It took all of his will power not to call her up and do that. He really, really, really wanted to lash out and crush her spirit; decimated her to the point where she could never connect with anyone, ever again. He would laugh as he heard her voice break and rejoice in her torment. He was in hell and wanted her to join him in the flame.

He wanted to, but would not. What would that prove? He was a male from a proper family and had always been taught to handle himself with dignity and class; something which most of the world simply did not have enough of.

He would have found this dichotomy interesting if they were not fighting for control of him at such a pivotal moment in his life. He knew that if the rage won, he would give her ammunition to use against him when she talked to others. She would say what an asshole he was and here was proof, saved on her telephone. Whereas if the class side won and he did not talk to her again, suddenly she would have much greater difficulty proving anything. The onus would be on her and he would come away with his head held high and dignity intact.

But what good is dignity when you are hurting as bad as he was? Dignity and class did not curl up to you in bed at night, and they sure as hell did not give you a hug and kiss when you see them. But then again, neither did she the last few times he saw her.

He was exhausted and wanted to sleep, but he knew that was just not going to happen. He hadn't slept since she gave him the knockout punch last night. All he could do was lay on his lumpy futon and gaze at the round light on his ceiling. His mind kept racing, trying to figure out what he did wrong and why things ended so badly. He had no answers and only more questions. He was in a daze and everything seemed distorted. Distant.

Was he going mad? He didn't know anymore. Just like she did not know if she still loved him. How could you not give someone that you had spent such a long time with an answer? She might have thought that she was sparing him an unpleasant truth, but it only served to anger him and feed the growing rage inside.

****

Ten weeks had passed and the only thing that had changed was the level of anger and resentment inside him. He had often wondered what the term "tasting one's own bile" meant, but now he knew for certain and did not relish it.

His face was constantly burning and he was certain that his blood pressure was dangerously high; all thanks to *her*. He refused to even mention the bitch's name because of the rush of rage that would wash over him every time he heard it.

At least he was back to being who he always was and would be. That whiny little wuss no longer existed

The best way he could describe the transformation was he had lulled himself to sleep, changing everything that made him who he was, all to try and satisfy a nasty piece of work that would never truly be happy.

Now he was awake.

He didn't like it.

Their "break" lasted three and a half weeks before he had broken down and called her to find out what was going on. He could not sleep. He could not concentrate on anything but her. She occupied his every waking thought, and with each of those thoughts came a stabbing pain at the very centre of his being. He had to know to answer.

Like before he wanted nothing more than to hurt her with his words, to make her experience everything that he had. He wanted to ruin her for the rest of her life.

He couldn't do it.

The conversation was brief and brutal.

He suggested that because he did not recognise the new person she had become since buying that piece of shit house, they should start over again.

He thought the relationship was worth fighting for.

She did not.

He could remember the iciness of her voice; the pure disinterest, disdain and utter contempt that was reserved for people that were below you.

Why she did that to him, he had no clue.

"Your friendship means a lot to me," she said, "And I think that we should remain platonic friends."

It was mean and uncalled for.

The rage hissed that she did not deserve to be treated fairly, but he replied, "Platonic? I don't like to deal with absolutes in life. You never know, perhaps someday if the stars align correctly, we could hook up again."

"That is definitely not going to happen, ever."

Not ever? Fuck you! Talk about over believing her worth! Sorry, but the sex really wasn't that great in the first place! Somehow over the years he had managed to convince himself that he cared for her so much that he was willing to overlook her sub-par performances for the sake of love. She truly was not good and she was the one who thought that she was doing him a favour by sleeping with him? Please! She was pathetic; it was like trying to hump a retarded mule. The only difference was the mule would put some effort into it!

The rage smiled inside his mind and he was about to release a tirade of obscenities aimed at her numerous insecurities when he stopped himself.

He had learned a long time ago that women require something to focus their aggressions toward men on. Without a specific comment or situation, they could not concentrate on one particular thing when bitching to their friends about what a terrible boyfriend he was.

The rage did not approve.

He controlled his voice and responded, "I agree. I think we are better as just friends. You mean a great deal to me and I would rather have you in my life as a friend than not at all."

This reaction caught her off guard. She had been expecting the nasty side of his personality that she had only heard about.

"Perhaps when I come to your city next, I could take you out for an ice cream to see how your life was."

There was dead silence on the other end of the phone.

He smiled and the rage smiled at his sneakiness.

"I would like that," she said, "We could hang out if you would like. We could even still talk to each other once every week or two to keep in touch."

Sure, then let me crush my balls in a vice.

"That sounds great. And there is one other thing I should probably tell you, because I guess it does not matter now."

"What's that?" she asked.

"Now I am not sure why I am telling you this."

Yes he was. She thought he was controlling before? Check this out. Fuck her.

"Telling me what?"

"Do you remember how I wanted you to come on a trip with me to the Highlands this summer?"

"Uh huh."

"Well, since neither of us had ever been, I wanted to make the experience an extra special one. So over the last two years I had been squirreling money away, putting every extra dollar I had toward a ring that would show you how much you meant to me. I was going to get down on one knee at sunset and ask you to marry me."

The bitch did not miss a heartbeat and said, "That would have been romantic."

Would have been romantic? Was that all she could say?

"Yes, it would have been."

Fuck you!

That was how the conversation ended.

He had not talked to her since.

He found out later that she had mentioned to one of his friends that the idea of him coming up to see her made her feel sick.

Him, make her feel sick?

She had no clue.

He was more pissed at himself than anything else. He had trusted the word of a woman that had no honour, no decency and no class. He had went against his instincts and it had cost him dearly.

She had planned this move for quite some time; of that he was certain. He knew something was in the works during his last visit, but had chosen to ignore his gut and having his heart ripped out was the cost.

It was a mistake he would never make again.

How could he ever trust anyone again?

How he hated her! How he loved her still.

Damn he was messed up.

At least the fates were on his side - for now.

He had been informed, on an almost weekly basis, about the series of unfortunate events that seemed to plague his now ex-girlfriend.

During their break, she had been written up at her second job several times and ended up quitting because she was getting burned out after working over seventy hours per week.

He told her, but she wouldn't listen. He had obviously been lying to her in an attempt to control her.

Later that week, not only did someone dent her car while she was at work, but shortly after her alternator died, both of which cost a pretty penny to repair.

The rage giggled.

The next week they had a major snowstorm and she did not bother to clean the snow off the dilapidated roof of her piece of shit house.

First she had water come through the ceiling of one of her spare bedrooms, and then the weight of the snow caused the drywall at the back of the house under the main roof supports to crack all the way down to the large bay window that overlooked her backyard.

She finally decided to get off her ass and pay someone to remove the snow from every part of the house except the peaked roof at the very front because there was not a great deal of accumulation there.

She went to work and came home to find that the snow she had not cleared had slid off of the roof and took all the tiles, rain gutters and siding from the front of the home with it.

She did an emergency patch job with tar, but not before the second bedroom on the main floor had water streaming down the walls and curling the drywall.

Yep, that was a great investment, wasn't it?

Stupid bitch.

The home inspector had told her that the roof need to be replaced within a year, but she ignored him and paid full price for the house because she thought it was cute.

To compound matters, her house insurance would not cover the repair costs to the inside of the house because her not replacing the roof is what led directly to all of her problems.

That and being a heartless cow.

Karma was a wonderful thing.

Conversely, ever since the break up, his luck had never been better.

He had won some money, started to work out, and most importantly, he had rediscovered the desire to write; something that had fizzled over the years with her.

The uncomfortable blue couch still taunted him on a daily basis with promises of comfort and support. But he knew better and sooner or later he would enjoy taking it into the backyard and burning it.

Still, it was on this couch that he received the best idea he had ever had for a story. It came to him in a dream, but the dream seemed more real than everything around him.

He had been in a familiar place, a cafe of sorts, and there were what appeared to be angels sitting at tables with ordinary people. Everyone was reading something and there were wonderful smells wafting through the air. It was the smells that stuck out in his mind the most because he could not remember ever smelling things in a dream before. It felt warm, pleasant and safe; almost like heaven.

He was about to wander around when a shirtless angel wearing assless leather chaps with a matching vest, leather cap, handlebar moustache, large gold earrings and thick gold chains appeared in front of him and smiled. In his hand he carried what appeared to be a daiquiri in a coconut shell with a tiny umbrella in it. The angel's lips did not move, but he distinctly heard a voice say, "It's good to see you Balthy, but it is not your time yet. We will talk about your role when you return."

Then he woke up back on the horrid, blue couch. He wrote down everything he could remember immediately because he knew he had stumbled upon something special. He wasn't sure what it was, but he had a feeling it would be a great story. He also knew that it would not have happened if she was still a part of his life.

That meant that everything in life happened for a reason, almost as if it were written in a movie script of sorts. Now that was an interesting concept. What if we were all actors in someone else's play?

But if that were the case, that meant that she was predetermined to shred his heart and he did not have a chance from the very beginning. So no matter what he did, no matter how hard he tried to make things work, if he were not part of her story, then there was nothing he could do about it.

In a way, that concept made the rage within lessen slightly, but in another, it truly sucked ass because he was powerless to stop it from happening. It was like knowing the answer to everything, but having nobody listening.

What if someone was reading everything that happened to him? What if he were just a character in a book that someone was reading? He was not proud of his past and had done things that nobody should ever know about. He was not sure he liked the idea of someone sharing the sum of his experiences, including this latest one with the bitch. Still, it might make for a good story.

That frame of thought made his head spin and he decided to not think about it for a while. It was something best left for a night of heavy beveraging with his friends.

His first story would be about his cousin, Mary, who had died a year earlier as a result of malnutrition brought on by surgery. He had some notes jotted down on a piece of paper and he used them to refresh his memory about the experience that was still all to recent for comfort.

He sat down in his favourite chair at the dining room table, took out a stack of lined paper and with a pen that he had "liberated" from work, began to write. It felt amazing to once again place his thoughts in ink and as the pen scratched along the paper, he felt the world around him begin to fade away.

There was nothing around him. All that existed was the connection between his mind and the words that appeared on the paper. He had tried to explain to people what happened when he wrote, but it was as difficult as a bird explaining how it felt to fly. It was special, unique and exhilarating all at the same time. When he wrote, for a brief moment in time, nothing else mattered.

It started slowly, but then like a dam bursting, the words flooded the pages. Line after line, page after page of text appeared in front of him, and for the first time in recent memory, he felt in control of his emotions.

The rage did not control him.

He felt calm, almost empty when he finally laid the pen down and massaged the palm of his right hand and fingers. He stretched and heard the bones in his spine crack loudly. God, he needed that.

He carefully gathered what he had written, tapped the edges on the table to even out the pages and then took a brief look at what he had just finished writing. It wasn't completed, not by a long shot, but it was definitely begun.

She died at the age of twenty-two, alone in a hospital room, unconscious in a dream that would now never end. Fifteen bags of different fluids were hooked up to her frail body in an attempt to open her collapsed veins and get vital nutrients to her dying organs. She held on for two weeks and I refused to believe she could die. How could she? She was only twenty-two.

Her name was Mary and she was my cousin. This is the story of her life.

I was supposed to meet both my parents and brother at the local gas bar on Sunday so we could take the two hour drive into Niagara Falls together, like a caravan of sorts, but when I arrived, only my parents were there. I guess my little brother, in an attempt to get his fiancé and two young daughters ready, didn't realise he had forgotten his wallet and identification at home until he had nearly reached us, a full hours drive. He had to turn around and drive back to his home, then come all the way back, plus an additional two hours on top of it.

I laughed.

The trip down was fast and I did my best to stay on the bumper of my dad's car, even though it was difficult to keep up with the magnificent speeds he reached along the highway. We saw several police officers, including two sneaky ones that were hiding on us. One was parked on the on-ramp and the other was standing on top of an overpass, aiming his radar at the cars passing below. I must admit, I found their choice of spots devious and strangely impressive, but in spite of their best efforts, they did not succeed in catching either of us.

We drove straight to my Aunt's house, picked her up and headed for the local funeral home.

Let me take a moment and explain to you my deep resentment, no, hatred of funeral homes. I truly despise them. Sometimes I think that hate is not a strong enough word to help illustrate my dislike of them. I loathe everything about them, from the lighting they use to the creepy way everything is so spotlessly clean.

There is always the thick smell of flowers that permeates the air, along with something else. It is more subtle, yet all too familiar. I can't quite place my fingers on it, but it is there, just below the surface, blending almost perfectly with the flora. If I close my eyes and concentrate, I believe I can still smell it.

It is one of those things that sticks with you, very distinctive, almost sinister; much like hospitals.

I hate hospitals almost as much as funeral homes. The environment is white, bright and incredibly sterile, both literally and metaphorically. The hallways have a disturbing echo to them and if you are ever admitted, there is a strong possibility that someone could have died in the bed you are resting in.

On every floor, people are suffering. You cannot rest or sleep soundly because every time you manage to fall asleep, you are woken up to be given your medications. I'm speaking from experience here.

It has been over twenty-five years since I was last admitted to the hospital for eye surgery. I was just a kid, but I still remember a nurse waking me out of a deep sleep to give me some sleeping pills to help me sleep! I kid you not! Or a personal favourite of mine was being turned over in the middle of the night to check my temperature - through my ass! Yeah, that was fun.

Hospitals suck, plain and simple. I've always believed that if you want to get sick, you should go to a hospital. Nothing good comes from those buildings, and once you check yourself in, there is a good chance you will never come out again.

But I digress, back to the funeral home.

It was a beautiful spring day and the sky was a deep, azure blue with fluffy, white clouds hanging around in the sky. The sun was shining brightly and there was a warm breeze that tickled the hair on my chin-length beard.

I had decided on my "Mafia look", which included a dark suit, white shirt, dark tie under my long, black overcoat. My hair was slicked back into a ponytail and beneath my shiny, black leather shoes I was wearing a pair of dark toe-socks complete with multi-coloured toes.

Now I know what you are asking yourself, why am I, a guy, wearing something that was designed exclusively for a female audience? The answer is simple: because they are cool. It feels like I am wearing gloves on my feet, and with my aptly named "monkey toes", it was a perfect match.

I love colours - the brighter and more vibrant, the better and I thought it would be amazing to wear such things on my feet. My first pair of toe-socks were rainbow coloured and each toe was a different, bright colour. I got them from my girlfriend for Christmas and I wore them until they fell apart.

They act as my little secret and make me feel better in stressful situations, like entering that house of despair.

I remember looking at the front of that building, with the hearse parked around the side, and shooting it the mental finger. Even now, I get tightness in my chest and I feel my breathing quicken as I think about it.

I truly, truly, truly hate them more than anything in life.

I didn't say anything, but I literally froze in my tracks. It took every ounce of willpower I could muster to follow my dad and aunt inside.

Instantly the smell brought back memories of every time I had entered a place like that.

The first funeral I had ever gone to was that of my uncle when I was a kid. That was soon followed by my Papa, Gun-nana and years later, my good friend's mom. They all had one thing in common, I didn't recognise the thing in the box. I still do not know what they did those people close to me, but whatever was laying there wasn't them.

I remember my father sitting my little brother and I down when we went to our first funeral and explaining to us what to expect. He told us that the person inside the coffin was cold, still and looked as though they were sleeping, and the purpose of seeing them was to be able to say good-bye. It made sense to me then, and I guess it still does today.

The only problem is that I refuse to have my last memory of that person be a sad one. I want to, and strive to, remember people as they were, not what they end up as. Maybe it is a selfish viewpoint, but it is my choice and I choose to remember a person's life, not their death.

In fact, when it is my turn to bite the big one, I want to be cremated immediately; none of this sticking around for several days while people hang over me and comment on how good I look, when in fact I look like shit. No way, not for me. Cremate me, slap my ashes in a shoe box and flush me down the toilet. Then have a photo of me at a local bar and get absolutely wasted in a magnificent party. I want loud music, good food, copious amounts of alcohol and no one in dark colours. I want people to celebrate my life and have a truly, memorably, good time.

I will give that funeral home credit because when I walked through those tinted, double doors, the place was fairly well lit and they had a cool, old hearse buggy against the left wall. It was roped off by silky, red rope and you could tell from the shine that somebody spent a lot of time waxing it.

There were darkened rooms on either side of the doorway and we walked past them and into the next room on the left. Immediately I saw my uncle, the long beard and bald head made him extremely recognisable. I always thought he looked like a member of Z Z Top, and before he decided to divorce my aunt, I enjoyed hanging out with him. He was what I like to call a "married confirmed bachelor". What I mean by that is even though he was married with four children, he never really acted like a father and continued to live his life as if he were still single.

I was the ring bearer at their wedding when I was just a little kid, and even then I remember thinking that something just wasn't right between the two of them. Eighteen years later I was proven right.

Now don't get me wrong, I do like the guy, but I can't help but think if he had paid a little more attention to his children rather than himself, Mary would still be alive today. See, it is difficult to put into words twenty-two years of neglect because it wasn't just one big thing, it was an entire series of things that are now virtually impossible to untangle

He did not want to end it there, but his eyes were getting tired and his hand was sore. Plus, he was hungry and did not know why until he looked at the clock. Six hours had passed since he started writing and it was well past dinnertime.

He didn't feel like cooking, so he thought it would be a good time to order a pizza from the place just up the road. He had been a regular there for years, but stopped when the ex-girlfriend started to give him the run around. It was their favourite spot and it had not seemed right to go there without her; there were too many memories for him to deal with.

But something about him writing again seemed to help put everything in perspective. Did he hate her guts and wish that she had never-ending cramps each month? Absolutely. Did he still love her more than anything in the world? For some strange reason, yes he did.

He missed the way she would spread her toes like a cat when he would massage her feet, or how soft her hair was when they would snuggle on the couch.

He was confused.

He knew it was over, but something inside screamed that it was just the end of the chapter, not the end of the story.

She did a number on him and he really did not know which end was up.

****

It had been two years since that fateful winter night when his world had changed forever. Who would have thought that after so much time, news of her could send his entire world into a tailspin? He should have been long over her, yet there he sat, alone, in the dark at the dining room table, staring into the smiling darkness.

It wasn't right.

She should not have that much of an affect on him.

Not now.

But she did and he could not understand why.

All things considered, his life had been going very well over the last three months. He was healthier than he had been in years; he had been going to the gym on a semi-regular basis and he could proudly say that he once again had a neck. He wasn't sure, but there was the chance that the beautiful redhead behind the counter was interested in him. She had legs that went all the way up, curly hair and seemed to always smell like cinnamon. He had even caught her staring at him out of the corner of his eye the previous week.

He had just about worked up enough courage to ask her out on a date when his best friend informed him on the deeds of his ex-girlfriend. He did not want to hear it, but something else made him listen. Perhaps it was the demon he was wrestling with inside his chest; the very same creature that interfered with his sleep, taunting him from the recesses of his subconscious with promises of peaceful dreams, and then churning the acid in his stomach into a frenzy so sleep was impossible.

He felt hurt, angry and somehow cheated. It bothered him that he felt that way and he did not understand why.

A long time had passed and he thought that she was part of his past. But wasn't that just like the past? Just as you think you have everything under control, something or someone reappears to kick you in the stomach. He smiled ruefully at the thought.

It was the story of his life.

He had never been able to win at anything. He tried so hard, but always came up that little bit short. Schooling, travelling, job hunting, it was all the same; he was close, but never close enough. Then there were relationships, the worst thing of all.

He had only had two girlfriends over his entire life and both had crushed his heart into dust; especially the last one. Not only did she turn his very core to ash, she set the remnants on fire and left only an empty shell behind. He had never been hurt like that before and had never allowed himself to be hurt like that again.

Now this.

Why did he tell him about her? It wasn't to be mean, of that he was certain. It was more out of shock and to probably tell him how lucky he was that she was not part of his life anymore.

Lucky, huh?

Was he?

He did not think so. He had always been a strong believer that if he was good and kept trying, eventually the universe would give him a break and he would finally make a difference, both to himself and someone else.

He'd been around for over three decades and the only thing that had happened was the darkness inside him had grown almost beyond his control. Now with this latest news, he did not know if he could hold on anymore.

His best friend had informed him that she had been whoring herself around her hometown up north. She had been meeting random men and then taking them back to her place for a one night stand! She had also been parking with other strangers and practising her oral communication skills on the beach, all of it without any form of birth control. Now she had met up with the most loathsome, cockroach of a man and was spending all of her free time with him and his two children!

He wasn't sure what was bothering him more: the fact that she was having copious quantities of unprotected sex with strangers in public, or that the thought of it filled him with jealousy and a strange sensation of anxiety.

He was not her keeper.

He had no business even caring about what she did with her life, no matter how stupid and asinine it was.

Yet, he still felt responsible for her. He had protected her from her family and everyone else while they were together and she repaid his kindness by crushing him when he least expected it.

He should take great pleasure in what she was doing because it meant only a short period of time before she became pregnant, if she were lucky, or picked up a sexually transmitted disease, if she were unlucky.

But he just couldn't do it.

What do you say to someone who you know is heading down the wrong path in life and they do not even realise it? How can you stop something from happening that the person is oblivious to?

He could understand her desire to be free and experience everything that life had to offer, but that was something that was done during the teenage years, not in your thirties. Now it seemed skanky and to quite honest, downright disgusting.

Where was the woman he had fallen in love with? He did not recognise this new, slutty creation that was systematically humping her way around the entire greater city area.

Did she believe that men were paying attention to her because of her looks? She was attractive, but that wasn't the reason.

Men were talking to her because she was easy and if they paid attention to her, there was a good chance they would get laid. That's it. Plain and simple.

How was he so certain of their intentions? That question was easy to answer. He knew because that was all that he had been after when he had started talking to her seven years ago.

She struck him as an easy lay and their first conversation had revolved around sex. He expected to get laid when they first met, and his hunch had turned out to be accurate. What he did not expect was to develop feelings for her.

If he had been able to get that acquainted with her upon their first meeting, why was he so shocked that she had reverted back to her old ways after he was no longer in the picture?

He had shown her another way and demonstrated that while sex was an important building block in the relationship, it was not the be all and end all.

It would appear that he was wrong.

Once a slut, always a slut.

You cannot turn a whore into a lady.

He should not be surprised that she had slept with ten men, not including her beach adventures, over the last three months.

He felt sick.

Why?

Why did it matter to him anymore?

He sat back in his uncomfortable chair, took off his glasses and rubbed his temples furiously in an attempt to dissipate the migraine that had formed.

He took in a deep breath, held it for a few moments and then let it out. It was an anti-stress technique he had read about in a magazine.

It didn't help.

His entire world had been turned upside down in an instant and he just didn't understand.

Did he still care for her?

Obviously! It was not possible to be part of somebody's life for that long and then suddenly feel nothing for them. Was that it? Was he still in love with her?

On some level, perhaps.

Was it jealousy over the sex that the other men were getting and he was not? That was possible, but it was something more. If it had been any other woman, his reaction upon hearing the news would have been, "That's great, thanks for sharing. I understand why men want a slice; it's good pie. I don't mind sharing as long as she saves a piece for me."

This was different.

Another sharp pain shot through his midsection and he grabbed his stomach as the flames grew stronger.

Should he call her? Was there anyway that he could warn her about what was coming? She would not believe him. In fact, she would not only ignore him, but convince herself that he was keeping tabs on her and claim that he was a stalker.

So what could he do?

He sighed loudly.

Nothing. He could do absolutely nothing. He was completely powerless and no other choice but to stand back and watch the woman that he had believed completed him, self-destruct.

He was going to say that now she had experienced more rubber than the highway, but that was not the case. Instead, he would have to say that she had now seen more shaft than an elevator.

He giggled and the dark funk which surrounded him momentarily lifted. Surely he could come up with at least one more analogy for her nocturnal adventures. He furled his brow and thought for a moment, then he had it. Gerri had now seen more balls than a tennis court. Yes. That was a good one. He laughed and then his imagination conjured up the image of her with another man. The darkness slammed down once more.

His mind was his own worse enemy. Every time the logical segment of his brain took over and made him realise that she was his past and he had to move on, the emotional side rose up like a tsunami and swamped it with feelings of rage, loss, hurt and betrayal.

She wasn't with him anymore and there was absolutely no chance of them getting back together. Even if there had been, after her latest display of brothel behaviour, he wanted nothing more to do with her. He felt disgusted by her lifestyle and suddenly had the urge to take a shower.

So, if he were so disturbed, why did he still care?

He shook his head and stretched. He was arguing in circles and it did not make a slight bit of difference. The one thing he was certain of was that hearing about her had stirred up a lot of things that were better left buried, locked away with the darkness inside his chest.

The darkness smiled.

Maybe sleep would help him gain a better perspective on things. It had always helped him before, so why should things be any different now?

What time was it, anyway? He looked toward the kitchen clock and noticed that it was nearly two o'clock in the morning. He had been sitting in the darkness, thinking about her for the last five hours and all he had to show for it was a splitting headache and stomach acid that was so strong, he was certain it could instantly dissolve an entire steak.

He pushed himself away from the table and stood up. He had been sitting for so long that his left knee refused to straighten and he nearly fell on the floor.

He had recently hurt his knee when he had foolishly decided to try and impress the redhead at the gym by squatting 500 pounds without warming up first. Yeah, she had been impressed alright, especially by the squeal of pain when he realised his kneecap was sticking out the side of his leg.

He needed surgery, but could not afford it. So he was left with letting his leg heal naturally, wrapped tightly in ordinary tape. It wasn't pretty, but it was all he could afford.

All he wanted to do was sleep and let the sweet oblivion of his subconscious immerse him in perpetual bliss. In his dreams he was someone special; someone that was not a loser and was finally able to win at the game of life.

He hobbled to his room and collapsed onto his futon that lay on the floor. People had always asked him why he did not buy a frame for the mattress, but he did not see the purpose in it. The futon was fine on the floor, no matter how "ghetto" it looked. That had been a bone of contention with the ex because she thought it looked cheap.

How is that for the universe having a sense of humour? A whore referring to something he had as being cheap.

There was the pain again and he had no bananas left to help eliminate the acid that was punching at the base of his throat.

Yep, he had to love that subconscious mind, always bringing his thoughts back to his ex-girlfriend. He laid on his back, closed his eyes and tried to force the thoughts of her back into the cage.

Sleep was a long time coming, and when it did, everything he had been repressing about her had free reign. Images upon images immersed his mind and he was powerless to stop them.

It was a beautiful day in the early summer. The sky was a pure blue and a squirrel was frolicking along the cement wall that lined the park. All the trees were bursting with green leaves that twirled mischievously in the light breeze, and his head rested on her lap while she played with his hair.

Her touch was soothing and he closed his eyes and smiled, while the bliss of the perfect moment engulfed his mind and made it still. No thoughts raced through his head, only peace.

"Do you want to know something crazy?" whispered Gerri.

Her voice seemed far away, as if it came from the far side of forever. He gave her hand a gentle squeeze and replied softly, "Sure."

"Have you ever thought that we were soul mates?"

He expected the familiar feeling of fear race up his spine; it has always happened when someone had mentioned anything to do with commitment, but this time the sensation was strangely absent. Instead, a warmth he had never felt before started in the exact centre of his chest and radiated outward until it filled his entire being.

It was a perfect moment.

Six months later he was alone.

He awoke with a jolt, sweat covered his torso and it felt like a giant hole had been ripped through his chest. He turned his head to look at the time; only thirty minutes had passed. This was not a good sign.

From the time he was a child, he had always had a terrible time sleeping, and as he had gotten older, the problem had intensified. Now it was not unusual for him to go twenty to thirty days with only cat-napping at night. It had reached the point that he was no longer certain of what was reality and what was a dream.

This was the worst he could remember. It had already been thirty-two days and he was on the cusp of finally sleeping when this had happened and now the end seemed all too far away.

Once while travelling through Europe, he became so tired that he actually thought he could taste colour. Even the unforgiving walls of a stone fortress seemed strangely soft and comfortable.

It was not good.

The worst part of being that tired was Death always seemed to take that opportunity to try and get him. He was not thinking metaphorically, but literally. He knew that he should not personify the fourth fate, but as far as he was concerned, Death had indeed been trying to get him for the better part of fifteen years, thus far unsuccessfully.

It had become a game after the seventh time he had thwarted Death's attempt to silence him forever, and he was getting quite good at it. In fact, he was undefeated; a very good thing because if Death managed to win only once, it was game over for him.

Recently, Death had become the most creative that it had ever been, but his "luck" had also been the best it had ever been, resulting in a score of 17-0. He had especially enjoyed the near-fatal crash on the highway just before his thirty-third birthday, ten months before.

He had been driving along the highway in the passing lane, going substantially faster than the posted speed limit in his fifteen year old car that was held together with strong tape and glue, when the unexpected happened. He felt something snap and then the front-right side of his car hit the asphalt as his tire shot off and skipped along the opposite side of the highway. Smoke and sparks followed his car as the axle dug into the roadway, and he somehow managed to turn the steering wheel enough so he could make it off to the left-hand shoulder of the road and came to a complete stop.

He could almost swear that he heard Death swear.

He got out of the car, looked at the damage and said, "Good one Death! You almost had me there! Unlucky!"

The tow truck driver asked him how he was still alive when he saw the damage because the accident had taken out both the upper and lower tie rods, ripped the drive axle out of the transmission and taken out both brake lines.

If he had been in the middle lane, where he had been only a few seconds before, the transport truck behind and beside him would have run over his little car and crushed both of them.

If he had been in the far right lane and had attempted to move the car to the right to get to the right shoulder, the broken axle would have dug into the ground and the car would have flipped down the highway and blown up.

He had been quite lucky.

But just like a perfect moment, everything comes to an end.

Since that incident, Death had tried to take him out eight more times; seven involved deer and once involved unknowingly breathing in toxic fumes for ten hours.

All in all, quite creative, but he was still here.

His eyes burned when he rubbed them with the heels of his hands. He yawned, stretched and tried to concentrate on the sensation of the cool sheets pressed against his naked form.

It didn't help. Sleep remained as elusive as the perfect cherry blossom. He was exhausted and the memories refused to leave him alone.

"Use your feelings as a measurement of mine," whispered Gerri, her small hands tracing the lines on his fingers. Her light touch sent shivers racing through his torso and he knew then and there that she was the only woman for him.

He stared deeply into her brown eyes and delicately caressed her cheek with his other hand. Her skin was soft and warm.

"I love you."

She smiled serenely and replied, "I love you too."

"Liar," hissed the darkness within.

She never loved him, never cared for him! All she had done was make him vulnerable to getting hurt and that is exactly what she had done. She had crushed his heart and damaged his spirit almost beyond recovery.

His stomach burned and the room spun around him. He had to do something to get his mind off her, so he reached for the pad of paper he had laying beside his bed and began to write. He had been told that it was good to get things off his chest by writing them down and then burning the paper, releasing the emotion back into the universe.

Personally he believed it sounded like a pile of crap, but at this point he was willing to try anything. He needed to sleep.

Things I have learned about life and love.

1. I learned that even though you could love someone with your entire being, it does not mean that they love you back. In fact, odds are that they are simply going through the motions.

2. Love is an illusion.

3. Happiness equals money which equals power which leads to happiness.

4. You can never rely on anyone other than yourself. If you do, you will be let down.

5. Emotions are for the weak.

He felt a bit better as he stared at the list. At least he now knew the truth; the darkness was right.

The beast smiled.

He made a mistake by trusting the wrong woman with his heart and it had cost him everything that made him strong. A huge piece of his heart was missing, leaving a void where she had previously occupied.

He could still remember how it felt the first time he had seen her with her new man. As soon as he laid eyes on the runt she had left him for, it felt like a surge of energy had ripped through his stomach and out the other side. He felt numb, like all sensations in the world had been torn away from him, leaving him completely exposed; vulnerable. He immediately wanted to crawl away somewhere dark, where the light of day was only a memory; somewhere he could recover and regain control of the emotions racing through his breast.

And he had crawled away, licking his wounds and waiting for the pain to subside. It had taken a long time for him to even raise his head in public and when he had finally found himself ready to face the world and perhaps begin to date again, he received news of the sexploits of the person that had meant so much to him.

Suddenly he was back at the beginning, dealing with emotions that had gained in strength by being stifled over time.

He wasn't sure how much more he could take. His mind was unravelling like a ball of yarn and he honestly did not know if he could wind it back up again.

"Enough!" he screamed to himself, "That's enough! I am tired of thinking about her. She obviously does not think of me, so I have to move on as easily as she has!"

He threw the sheets off his sweaty form and placed his feet on the yellow carpet beside his bed. He took another deep breath and slowly let it out as he ran his fingers through his rapidly thinning hair.

Yeah, he especially liked how his hair was not only going white, but also rapidly thinning on top. Great genetics. He figured that he would be white and bald within three years at most. While he was certain that he would remain as attractive as he always had been, part of him couldn't help but believe that growing his hair out for charity had been a mistake.

Several years before, after getting screwed out of another full time job, he decided to try and increase his chances of getting into heaven by growing his hair out for charity; it might not help, but he was certain that it couldn't hurt his chances, especially with all the wrong he had done in life.

The charity was called Locks of Love and they made wigs for children with cancer. The hair had to be a minimum of twelve inches long, as it was with most things in life, because it had to be able to be cut and styled for the individual.

He had beautiful hair that was always very soft and shiny. He took good care of it and used only the best products on it, but even then, the longer it became, the more that would be left in his brush after his morning shower. After two years of growing, he cut off all of his hair and shaved his head. The result was a large ponytail of deep blond hair for the kids and a head that had substantially less hair remaining than before he began.

It was all for a good cause and they had mailed him a certificate of appreciation for his efforts. He was proud of it and had a copy hanging on the wall of his cubicle right beside his favourite song lyrics.

Maybe that was why she left him; it was just after shaving his head. Maybe it was the ninety pounds he had gained while they were together. Was she disgusted by the curtain of flesh that hung down from his belly? If that were the case, at least he might have done something about it before it was too late. After the split, he had lost all the weight he had gained and was now in the best shape of his life.

But deep down he knew the real reason why she had left him, and it was something that was more than likely responsible for his present frame of mind. It was the sex. He was too large for her.

In spite of his best efforts to be gentle, every time they had sex, she would swell shut tighter than a whore's legs in church. Oh, he liked that analogy. He grabbed a piece of paper and wrote it down before he forgot about it. Now where was he? Oh yes, the sex thing.

Every time they had sex, she would get hurt and she managed to keep that from him for several years. That is what hurt more than anything else, the lies. He had always been very strong physically and was paranoid about accidentally hurting someone. He had always been extremely careful when holding her hand or handling his new-born nieces, so when she had finally told him that he had been hurting her for years, it hit him like a body blow.

She had informed him that having sex with him hurt so much that she had started to dread seeing him because she knew they would inevitably end up in the bedroom. Apparently it had become so bad that her sex drive had vanished completely and during their last few times together, she was merely going through the motions.

She could not have hurt him more if she tried. Hurting someone he cared about was his greatest fear and it turned out that in spite of being as gentle as he could, he hurt the person that meant everything to him.

It wasn't his fault that he was well endowed. Society had always implied that women were searching for a man of girth, but that truly wasn't the case. He wished that she had said something so they could keep trying different things until she found something that suited her body type. Instead, he brought pain to his angel.

After hearing her explain why she was not interested in sex anymore, he became paranoid about sleeping with other people because he did not want to hurt them.

Now, the woman that was his world, was out sleeping with everyone and not him. In a way, it was a good thing. At least she discovered that she liked having sex again, and her sex drive had returned with a vengeance. He should feel happy for her, but deep inside he was extremely jealous of the entire situation. He felt cheated and insulted that she seemed to have no problem humping other men, but he had destroyed her sex drive. That didn't seem fair. He knew that all other partners would be compared to him, but that did not make it any easier to deal with the idea that she was acting as the bun for a factory of sausages.

It felt dirty.

So, that is what was bothering him. It was a territorial thing. She had decided that he was unworthy of her time and efforts and was searching for the man who would father her children.

For the longest time he had believed that to be him.

Now he had nothing.

He was alone.

He felt lost and only she had the ability to lead him home.

No she didn't. Not anymore.

He shook his head and tried to make the hurt go away; to force it back into its cage, but to no avail. The darkness was free and enjoying itself at his expense.

The darkness was him.

Was he beginning to lose himself, or was he finally finding himself? Only the rage knew and it merely giggled at his predicament.

What was going on? He was talking about himself in the third person sense; that couldn't be a good thing.

He looked at the clock, three-thirty. The middle of the night. He needed to get some air and try to work off some anxiety so he could sleep, if only for a few hours.

He knew that he really shouldn't be walking the streets in his neighbourhood during the early hours of the morning, but he felt relatively safe. Everyone in the area knew who he was and generally left him alone.

He had moved to this area several years before and only found out about its reputation after signing a lease with his landlord. Apparently the previous tenants of this townhouse were all women and one of them had a tiny car that she parked in the driveway. One night, the local kids picked up her car, moved it to the nearby field and burned it.

Several months after that, they had tried to break into the house by setting the trim around the doorway on fire. That explained why the door did not match anything else on the house.

The roughest thing he had ever seen was the previous summer while he was out back barbecuing hamburgers. He saw this man sprint down the road, followed closely by a car that cut him off. Another man jumped out of the vehicle, grabbed the first man by the shirt and shouted, "Where's my money? Where is it?" Then he head butted the runner!

The gentleman from the car had turned and looked at him, to which he threw his shoulders back and said, "What?"

The guy looked as though he were thinking about something, then turned his attention back to the man on the ground.

It was a rough area, but the kids were good. They just did not have the necessary parental supervision. He had been a troublemaker when he was young, and that was with both parents keeping tabs on him. He could not imagine what he would have been like if one or neither of them were there.

These were good kids, they just needed someone to show them what was right from what was wrong. He was in the process of setting up a community drop in centre, so they would have somewhere to go rather than hang out on the street corners. With any good luck, it should be up and running within a few weeks. It would make a huge difference in this community.

He put on his comfortable sports jersey, a pair of old, cut off jeans, his sandals and headed out the door. A wave of heat caught him off guard and he had to stop and give his eyes a moment to adjust to the darkness.

There were streetlights, but they had not worked for years and this area was not a high priority for the city to fix up, so everything was encased in blackness.

The midsummer night air was thick and the smell of flowers hung over everything like a fog. Only a few stars could be seen because of the glow of light from the nearby city core. It was a pity because he had always liked watching the stars at night. It was peaceful and gave him hope that this life was not all it seemed; that perhaps, just perhaps he was a part of a larger story.

He used to believe in a great many things: happiness, joy and especially love. Now he believed in nothing except the hole in his heart. It was real, tangible and jagged around the edges.

The only story he was part of was the one that his ex-girlfriend was telling to her friends.

His sandals felt squishy under his feet as he strolled to the end of his street and stopped. Which way? Towards the park or the river? Toward the park. He turned left and headed toward the nearby park. There wasn't much left of it now, just a few rusty swings, a broken slide and half of a teeter totter. The foliage was unkempt and knee high weeds covered the entire area. It seemed almost post-apocalyptic, which was a sad statement considering the time they were living in when gap between the haves and the have nots was at its smallest in history.

All someone had to do was....

His train of thought was interrupted as he came around the corner and saw a group of five shadows circling something on the ground. As he moved closer, he saw it was the naked form of a woman.

His heart jumped into his throat and he shouted, "Hey! What are you doing?"

Several figures heads shot up like a prairie dog and they glared at him. All of them were dressed in dark clothes, so all he could see was the whites of their eyes. One of them shouted back, "Nothing for you to see here, man. Keep moving if you know what is good for you."

"Come on guys," he said, moving closer with his palms extended toward them, "You don't want to do this. I've seen nothing. Just let the lady go and get out of here."

"Now there is where you're wrong," replied another voice, it was the man currently between the woman's legs. "See, we really do want to do this. This bitch wants to take us all, over and over again. Maybe she will even take you as well. What do you think? You want to take him after all of us?"

The man lowered his head and slowly licked the side of the woman's face, tasting the saltiness of the tears that streamed from her eyes.

"No thanks, I'm good," he replied, still moving closer. The woman looked strangely familiar, but where did he know her from?

"In that case, get the fuck out of here before we make you our next bitch."

The man made a good point. He did not know this woman or the situation he stumbled across. Perhaps she had opted to have a gang bang in the middle of the park. He did not know. Why should he get involved? It wasn't his fight.

Yet he knew he had to do something. He had been raised to protect those around him, especially women, and even though modern society frowned upon such barbaric viewpoints, he could not stand by and do nothing. He moved closer.

The woman looked familiar.

"You make a good point. I wouldn't want to be your next bitch, but the problem is that I can't do nothing unless I know that she is fine."

She looked very familiar.

"What are you? Some kind of hero? I'll tell you what, you have huge balls, I'll give you that, so I'll make this easy on you. Tell the man you are loving this."

The man grabbed the woman by the back of her hair and raised her up so she could look directly at him. His hips never stopped moving as he snarled, "Tell him."

His heart dropped.

It was Gerri.

"Gerri?" he muttered, "Gerri, is that you?"

The woman opened her swollen eyes and whispered, "Bear? H-help."

"Oh, you know each other? Good, it will make things less awkward. Give me just another minute and then she's all yours."

He moved forward, a huge ball of fear gripping his chest. "Let her go! Now!"

All five shadows disengaged themselves from Gerri and moved forward as one to intercept him. When one of them reached into their front pocket, his bouncer instincts took over and he immediately balanced on the balls of his feet.

This wasn't good; outnumbered five to one, while the sixth continued to pump and watch the situation.

It had been a very long time since he had been in a fight and never before in one that had so much on the line. He brought up his hands and assumed a defensive stance, with one leg slightly behind the other.

This wasn't good at all. He was out of practice and they had the gleam of bloodlust in their eyes. This could be his last fight.

They figures took up their positions and then in a blink of an eye, swarmed him like ants on honey. Everywhere he looked, another fist or foot was coming at him. He did his best to block them, but there were too many and he fell to one knee. This sign of weakness only strengthened their resolve and they redoubled their efforts to curb stomp him into the next life.

As he did his best to protect his head, he happened to glance toward Gerri. Her face was badly bruised and her lips were split and bleeding as her attacker relished the show. Just as he felt himself ready to pass into unconsciousness, Gerri opened one of her eyelids and locked an eye with his. He saw pain beyond measure reflected there and a fire of defiance that still burned brightly within.

If she had not given up, neither would he.

The rage burned inside him, its claws darting out between the bars of the cage that had served as its prison for so long. Yes, it screamed, let us out!

The darkness smiled.

The cage door burst open and the beast was released.

Everything went into slow motion.

One hand shot out and grabbed the nearest attacker between the legs. He felt something soft and spongy and crushed it. He heard a satisfactory shriek.

All his life he had been worried about his strength, about accidentally hurting people. No longer. Gerri had shown him what true strength was.

He snarled and burst to his feet, the rage pulsating like fire through his veins. He balled up a huge fist and brought it slamming downward into the nose and cheek of another attacker. He felt the bone shatter under the onslaught and revelled in the crimson flow that sprayed across the air. It was rather beautiful.

He immediately kicked backward and came in contact with the third person's kneecap that splintered like a sledgehammer hitting a popsicle stick.

God, this felt good! They all deserved pain! His pain!

He whipped around, blocked a punch that was coming at him, grabbed the wrist of his attacker and brought his flat palm smashing into the elbow. The person may have screamed when the bone burst through the skin of his arm, but he did not know because all he could hear was the wave of the beast that now controlled him.

Something hard smashed against his side and he felt the distinct snap of a few ribs. He smiled and looked toward his fifth attacker who had found a tire iron and had hit him with it. He licked the blood from his lips, admiring how it tasted, and then he drew his foot back and brought it upward between the legs of the attacker with all the strength he could muster. He felt something explode like a rotten tomato being thrown at the sidewalk and the attacker dropped to the ground, holding himself. But before a single cry came, he drew back and soccer-kicked him right in the jaw.

He was about to kick him again when he felt something invasive and looked down in wonderment at the blade sticking out of his chest.

He felt rough whiskers on the left side of his neck and heard someone whisper, "Forgot about me, didn't you?"

He couldn't move. The man's breath smelled sour and his dark eyes seemed all too familiar. He gasped as the knife was removed and plunged into his back five more times.

"You put up more of a fight than any of us expected, but you are still only one man. You could have just walked away, but you just couldn't leave well enough alone. Now you are going to die, and for what? That whore? Stupid mistake."

The man plunged the knife into his back one more time and he sagged to his knees. It was difficult to breathe. He was certain the knife had taken out one of his lungs and most of his other vital organs. He looked down and saw deep purple blood pooling around his body. Strange, he always thought that blood was red.

The man grabbed him by the jaw and leaned in so they were eye to eye. "Now, I am not an unmerciful man, so I'll tell you what I am going to do for you. I'm going to kill that pretty little woman over there and you are going to watch. Then, when I think you have suffered enough, I will finish you off. I'll even let you decide how you want to die. What do you say?"

He tried to talk, but all he could manage was a gurgle. The man slapped his face playfully, walked over to Gerri's prone body and slammed the knife through her chest and directly into her heart. Her eyes opened wide and she screamed.

It cut though the haze that surrounded his dying mind and drove him into action. He gathered up all the strength he had remaining and launched himself at the man who had taken away everything from him.

"Now what about yo...."

He slammed into the man before he could finish his thought and they tumbled to the ground. He reached up and wrapped a hand around his attackers throat. He could feel the rings of cartilage and pressed his thick fingers around each side and squeezed with all the strength he could muster.

The man gasped, wrenched the knife from Gerri's body and brought it repeatedly downward.

There was no pain. He did not feel the sharp metal of the blade pierce his flesh again and again. All he was aware of was the death grip he had on the man's throat. He squeezed harder and felt the rings collapse under the pressure of his hand.

The man's face was turning bright red and the knife stabs were slowing down as he began to suffocate. Finally, the knife stopped moving, as did the man's chest, and with one final surprised gurgle, death came calling.

He gave the man's throat one last squeeze to make certain he was dead, then rolled off him and crawled toward Gerri's naked body. She did not move.

He was fading out, he could tell. Everything seemed distant and yet more real than anything had ever been before. The rage was gone, exhausted and replaced by a sense of peace.

He looked at the naked form of the woman that he loved and who had broken his heart. In spite of all the bruises and marks, she was still beautiful to him. She was his angel in life and now he hoped that she was one in the afterlife. She deserved it. He was sorry that he wasn't the man she had wanted, but he secretly hoped that in the last second of her last breath, she had found that which made her the happiest. If only it were him.

If only.

He could hear sirens in the distance that were getting closer. It was too late for him; he didn't think he had any blood left. And it was definitely too late for her. He had failed her once more.

He couldn't save her. He tried, but couldn't stop something bad from happening to her. He wasted his life.

He couldn't let them find her like this. With great difficulty, he pulled off his blood soaked jersey and laid it the best he could over her body.

Puncture marks littered his torso, and as he lay down beside her, his breathing began to slow.

He smoothed the matted hair away from Gerri's face, gently kissed her forehead and collapsed beside her in the grass.

ACT FIVE

The grass was damp with the combination of early morning dew and his blood. It stuck to his face and felt cool against his skin. Normally he would have relished the sensation, but this time it was the furthest thought from his mind.

He felt his breathing slow and knew that he was about to die.

Strange. He was a highly educated man and had read the literature from all of the world's religions, yet the reality of what was happening to him was unlike anything he had ever come across. Sure, there were a few similarities, but this was a truly unique experience. It was too bad he had to die to experience it.

His body felt heavy, like lead, and he could no longer move his fingers. His body was shutting down and nothing would restart him. His eyes were dry, but he was afraid that if he were to blink, he would never open his eyes again.

So this was death. Huh. He had never believed in the whole "light at the end of the tunnel" thing, but secretly he had hoped he was wrong and there were angels waiting to take him to heaven.

Oh yeah, it was too late for him. He had forgotten. He had done so many things in his life that he was not proud of, that his acceptance into eternity was a long shot at best and laughable at worst.

Still, if there was a heaven he hoped both Gerri and Mary had found it. Mary was an innocent and Gerri, while the cause of so much pain in his life, had found something to love in him, if only for the briefest moments of time.

His eyes stopped focusing and he knew it would all be over soon. The darkness would come and he would not feel anything ever again. His one main regret was being unable to dance with his nieces at their wedding. Still, maybe the universe would grant him the opportunity to look in on them from time to time.

"I'm sorry, Balthy, but that is not the way things work."

Did he just hear a voice?

"Of course you did, silly! It's me, Tim!"

Tim? What? Where are you?

"I'm right here beside you."

What do you want?

"I was so impressed by your performance that I had to come and get you myself. I'm here to take you home."

"Are you death?"

"Yes I am, though not that of the party! You must try one of Mikey's Cinnamon Squirrels! I'm telling you, when you drink three of them you will be acting like a nut! Oh, that is so bad!"

Cinnamon Squirrel? Mikey? What are you talking about? I'm confused? Where is the tunnel with the light at the end of it? Where are the angels?

"What do you think I am? I'm the Angel of Death, Greetings and I make an excellent quiche, though my crème Brule is nothing to scoff at! As for the tunnel, it is under construction at the moment. We are making a few changes and bringing it up to date. You know, giving it a much needed make over."

Are you taking me to heaven or hell?

"Neither. You don't need to go to your version of heaven. In fact, I'm taking you back to where your adventures began, at my cafe. I have a table reserved for you."

The cafe? Like the one in my dream?

"Exactly like the one in your dream. Let me tell you what a surprise it was having you suddenly appear like that. I cannot remember the last time a soul was strong enough to make a guest appearance so early in their career."

Why can't I see you?

"You will. Very soon."

I'm scared.

"Don't be. Everything will be fine, I promise. It's almost time."

He could feel his heart slowing. It beat once more then stopped.

"Let go of your last breath and relax. Feel yourself sinking into a warm bath."

He did as he was told and suddenly everything went silent.

It felt strange not breathing, but he was not worried because the chill of the early morning was gone from his body and he felt warm and safe.

Will it take long for us to get there?

"No. In fact, here we are."

A gentle breeze caressed his naked back and the rich smell of summer filled his senses with peace. He felt his chest moving and slowly his eyes adjusted to the soft, glowing light surrounding him. He started to move and expected to feel the pain from his stab wounds, yet there was none.

"You are healed, Balthy. There is no pain here and no suffering, unless you include being forced to dress in the previous season's fashions. Don't get me started about fabrics! I get all frazzled and then Antoine will truly have his work cut out for him."

"Who is Antoine?"

"My personal masseuse with strong hands and the body of a Greek God. In fact, he used to be one. Go on, you can stand up."

He gradually brought his knees under his torso and tentatively got to his feet. The glowing light receded and he found himself in the middle of a lush, green meadow that was swaying slowly in the warm breeze. A vibrant Amarillo sky with white, cotton candy clouds seemed to stretch on forever.

He looked down at his chest and touched where the knife had invaded his body time and again, yet there was not a single mark. His skin was as smooth and flawless as that of a new-born.

"See, you are as good as new."

He felt a grip of iron on his shoulder and turned around, expecting to see a monster of a man. What he saw instead was an average sized man with fine, porcelain-like features and the straightest, fullest head of shoulder length hair he had ever seen. It was as black as a starless night and seemed to shimmer with an almost blue colour. He was clean shaven and was dressed in a paprika coloured, long sleeved, button down dress shirt, a pair of perfectly pressed taupe slacks and black leather sandals. Folded neatly behind him was a pair of wings covered in white feathers the colour of blowing snow.

He was, for the lack of a better word, beautiful.

"Why thank you very much, Balthy! You make me blush!" said Tim, playfully averting his eyes.

"You can read my mind?"

"Of course I can! We are in heaven, anything is possible!"

"Wait a second. I thought you said that you were not taking me to heaven? And why do you keep calling me Balthy? My name is..."

Tim held up his hand and said, "I did say that, but it is not what you think. This is heaven, but not the one you thought it was."

"What?"

"See, heaven is a concept that all the people of the earth share. It has always been that way since the very first script was written, and we have done our best to ease the transition of death by creating various quarters around town."

"Quarters? Like neighbourhoods?"

Tim smiled, "Exactly. Every religion throughout time has their own quarter just over there."

Tim pointed vaguely in the direction of where the earth met the sky and continued with the wave of his hand. "See, people believe so strongly in a certain afterlife, that it would rude of us not to provide one, just as they think it should be. For example, we have a Mayan Quarter and even an Ancient Greek Quarter, complete with Fates. Let me tell you, they truly know how to throw a party! I have two words for you: Bacchus Festival! By the way, how do you feel about nudity?"

"Nudity? Bacchus Festival? What are you talking about?"

Tim's hands flicked around dramatically and he replied, "I'm so sorry! I forgot that you just got back, but you will understand everything soon. And to answer your next question, yes, there is a Christian Quarter, complete with clouds and scores of angels singing in robes that were flattering thousands of years ago. Don't get me started about their choice of outfit. I mean would it kill them to put some colour on once in a while? All I am asking for is a hint of strawberry on the fringes of their outfit. That's it! But from their reaction you would think that I had suggested everyone should go on a diet or something! But just between you and me, once you have two bums rather than one, I think there is an issue! I'm so bad!"

He smiled and said, "Yes, you sure are. Anyway, why am I not with my family and friends in the Christian Quarter?"

Tim rolled his eyes and sighed.

"OK, let me give you the condensed version. When people die they go to their particular afterlife for as long as it takes for them to realise."

"Realise what?"

"To realise that heaven is much more than a particular nationality because everyone is a national of heaven. It gets complicated, but all souls *are* everything and will eventually be everywhere. There is no difference between genders and skin colours. When this is realised, they return to the Cafe for their next role. You, my dear Balthazar, seem to be the exception to the rule because you always return directly to the Cafe. This is quite unusual. You must be something special."

"I used to think so, but the women in my life would tend to disagree. And please stop calling me Balthazar."

"But why would I want to do that? It is your name! You are Balthazar and not only have you have been to earth several times already, but you have also taken on some roles that are so difficult that they are reserved for our most elite actors. I know you don't believe me, so there is only one way to fix things. I'm famished, let's grab a bite to eat and we can talk some more."

"Where can we grab a bite to eat? There is nothing around here but wide-open meadowlands. I don't see a single building for miles, let alone a cafe."

"You are so cute! Look behind you."

He turned around and found himself staring at a beautiful cafe, complete with wooden pillars, oversized chairs and ornately carved tables. He could not tell how large the cafe was, but it seemed to go on for vast distances and yet none at all. It was really strange, but the one thing that was constant was the vast numbers of people sitting around laughing and talking with each other. The most amazing part for him was seeing angels everywhere sitting with people as if it were an everyday occurrence. It was then he realised that in heaven, it was.

He stared with a mixture of shock, happiness and excitement and the mass of people. It was amazing and he even thought he saw people he knew, but from where he had no idea.

"You do know them, Balthy," said Tim from behind a nearby table where he had sunk down unceremoniously into one of the large chairs. "Not from this last lifetime, but from your previous ones. See, everyone you meet in each of your lives is a person you have known before. Travelling to the earth always makes me famished. I could eat an entire tub of double chocolate brownie ice cream, covered in whipped cream and chocolate sauce! But I suppose I have to be good. It's almost swimsuit season.".''

"Are you serious?" he replied, joining Tim at the table.

"Absolutely! Have you ever met somebody for the first time and taken an immediate, active dislike in them?"

He nodded his head.

"There you go. You remember them from a previous life, even if you don't think you do. Sometimes you will deal with the same people over and over again, especially if you play off each other so well."

He had a sinking feeling in the pit of his stomach when he said slowly, "Gerri?"

Tim smiled like the proverbial cat who got away with eating the mouse and replied, "Gerri? Why yes, as a matter of fact, you have worked together several times in the past. Her real name is Cera."

His face must have said it all because Tim quickly motioned and a two large bowls of steaming cappuccino appeared in front of them.

"Now Balthy, before you go and fly off the handle, take a drink and you will understand everything."

He wasn't thirsty. A surge of pure, hot, rage shot through his body at the thought of being forced to "work" with his ex for all of eternity. The vein in the middle of his forehead was pulsating and he could feel the muscles in his jaw clenching.

"She is here?"

"Yes, quite close actually and I would be glad to introduce you, but not until you have had something to drink."

He tilted his head ever so slightly to the side and said, "I would like that. There are several things we should discuss."

"Balthy! Are you going to behave? You look like a cooked lobster."

He smiled like a snake about to eat the unsuspecting rat and whispered, "Of course I will behave. Why should I be angry toward her? I mean just because I wanted to spend my entire life with her, only to have my heart shattered into a thousand pieces and then burned to ash, means nothing. I died horribly trying to save her when I should have just turned and walked away. So why should I be upset? Nah, I just want to talk to her, that's all."

"You know you cannot lie in heaven, right? I know you are hurt, but be careful what you say because words can have a long lasting affect up here."

"I would not lie to you, Tim. You seem like a great guy and I would not want to make your life difficult. So, let me take a quick drink and then you can reintroduce us. Is that chocolate on top of the froth?"

Tim smiled and nodded, "Of course! It just wouldn't be the same without it!"

He reached down and grasped the large vessel of liquid and brought it up to his lips. As soon as the deliciously warm liquid entered his mouth, his mind exploded with knowledge. Suddenly he understood everything; he remembered everything. All of his past lives came rushing back to fill the corners of his mind that he did not even know he did not know about.

He blinked rapidly and looked with new eyes upon his friend who smiled warmly at him.

"Hello again Tim! I'm sorry I didn't remember what you looked like, but part of me recognised the smell. Is that strawberries and cream you are wearing?"

"It is! I'm trying new shampoos and conditioners. If you like this one, you should have smelt the mango, papaya, peach blend I had before this. It was absolutely scrumptious!"

"I bet it was. And by the way, you are looking good! Those spa treatments are working well for you, so whatever you are doing, keep it up."

"Oh, Balthy! Behave! Don't you know that flattery will get you everywhere?"

He smiled and was about to say something else when he heard a voice coming from behind him that set all the hairs on his neck on end and twisted his colon.

"Hello Bear."

Balthazar turned around slowly and locked eyes with Cera, the single person who had brought so much discomfort and hurt to his lives.

"Hello Cera," he replied icily, "It is good to see you managed to find your way back here. What do you want?"

His reactions seemed to catch her off guard and she stammered, "I just wanted to talk with you about what happened between us."

"Now why would you want to do that? Did something happen between us?" growled Balthazar.

Cera's demeanour changed to mirror Balthazar's and she said, "I guess not. Is there anything you would do differently if you could do it all over again?"

"Yeah, there is. I'd never allow myself to trust another woman and fall in what I thought was love - it hurt too much."

Tim moved quietly in his chair and watched with keen interest at what was playing out in front of him.

Cera's eyes narrowed and she said, "You can't go your entire life not allowing people into your heart."

"Yes I can," replied Balthazar, a slight snarl in his voice as his face darkened. "Every time I have, I have gotten burned. It's my own fault for allowing you to get too close."

Cera looked as though she had been slapped and said, "In all fairness, I was quite persistent."

"Yes you were, and when I finally opened up and let you in, you didn't like what you saw and crushed me! Yeah, like I want to experience that *ever* again!"

"That's not what happened, Bear! I..."

"Shut up!" screamed Balthazar, "I don't want to hear your lies! You screwed me over without a second thought, plain and simple! Tim, can you please shut her up?"

Tim started to take a breath when Cera interrupted him. Her eyes were blazing like miniature suns and she yelled, "Don't you dare tell me to shut up! I am not one of your friends that you can intimidate! You don't know what happened!"

"Oh, but I do!" snarled Balthazar as he leaned forward in much the same way as a wolf about to pounce upon an unsuspecting deer. "You used me for years and when I finally worked up enough courage to talk to your father about marrying you, you dumped me out of the blue with some bullshit excuse about soul searching!"

Cera locked eyes with Balthazar and did not back down an inch. When she spoke, her words hung in the air like icicles, "I loved you."

"Along with most of the north."

"Kiddies, kiddies, that's enough. Stop right there."

If they heard Tim, they gave no indication.

"Fuck you," said Cera, her voice cracking.

"I did and got frost bite on my dick, you frigid bitch! Die alone!"

His words hit her harder than any physical blow could and she whispered, "I did."

Balthazar was about to say something else when Cera turned and stormed away. He felt good about himself, that he was finally able to purge his hurt toward the entity that caused it. He didn't notice the tears streaming from her eyes.

He turned back toward Tim who was shaking his head sadly.

"What? She deserved it!"

Tim smiled ruefully and said, "You just don't get it, do you?"

"Get what? That she is a worthless cow that hurt me in more ways than I deemed possible? Or how about how she slept her way around most of the known world? She was a whore!"

"So were you," replied Tim.

"That's not the point! She left me broken and alone without a second thought!"

"Do you really think that you did not cross her mind ever again? What if I was to tell you that there were several times when she picked up the phone to call you, but decided not to because of how she had hurt you?"

Balthazar stuck out his bottom lip in though and said slowly, "Even if she did, why didn't she try to come and see me? I would have been angry, but I still would have listened to her! She never tried!"

Tim sighed and said, "What do you think she was doing in that neighbourhood at that time of night?"

The truth of Tim's words cut through his rage like a knife and suddenly he realised the mistake he had just made. He turned and was about to go after Cera when Tim said, "You can't do anything about it now, Balthy. Cera has just been assigned a new role and won't be back for a while. Remember, sometimes things are not always what they appear to be."

"Ain't that the truth," agreed Balthazar, "At least things couldn't get any worse."

"Why hello Tim. Hello Balthazar." said Elley, appearing from behind a nearby pillar and walking toward their table. She wore a tight, black dress that matched her stiletto heels and her curly red hair hung in waves past her shoulders and around her raven black wings. Her eyes were as piercing green as her skin was white and she locked them directly on Balthazar.

"Speaking of frosty, hello Elley," said Tim, as he crossed his legs and tilted his head to the side. "I see that staying off your feet has done you the world of good. How is your back holding up?"

Elley gave Tim a surly smile and replied, "Very well, thank you. You know, it is so unusual to see *a man* sitting like that with his legs crossed. Is it comfortable?"

Tim pursed his lips and quipped, "It is. I would suggest you try crossing your legs once in a while, but I would not want to interfere with your social life."

Elley shot Tim a death look which was returned immediately.

"Anyway, I thought I should come by and say how impressed I was by your latest performance, Balthazar. I was heart broken when I saw what Cera did to you!"

Balthy shuffled uncomfortably at the memory of the experience and his latest conflict with Cera. He despised her and hoped never to work with her again.

Elley did not blink and continued to stare right through him as she continued, "It wasn't right. You loved her with everything you were and still she disposed of you like a piece of junk. Still, you tried to save her from that group of men and what did it get you? Killed. Have you even had a happy role yet?"

Balthazar shook his head.

"That doesn't seem right to me. I mean, here you are, obviously one of the most talented actors they have and what roles are you assigned? A whore, a professor, a loser and a writer? What's next? A bum? That is four roles that dealt with nothing but disappointment, anger and pain. Don't you think you deserve something better?"

"There were some great moments in those roles. They weren't all bad."

The very corners of Elley's mouth turned up and she said, "That's right. There were a few brief moments of happiness, but do they make up for lifetimes of pain? Have you ever wondered what the writer was thinking?"

"Careful Elley," said Tim, the slightest hint of a snarl in his voice.

Elley glanced quickly over at Tim who had uncrossed his legs and was leaning forward with his hands resting on his knees. Elley licked her lips and turned her attention back to Balthazar.

"All I am saying is I believe in your acting ability and think you deserve the chance at happiness. That's all. I would love to have you come work for us."

"Elley," cautioned Tim.

"Just think about it. Maybe something could be arranged on a limited basis, perhaps for a single lifetime. That way you can tell that I am not lying to you. Anyway, I have to go! Ta! Ta! I will see you soon, Tim."

Tim's eyes became as hard as diamond as he replied, "I look forward to it, Elley."

Elley winked at Balthazar and then disappeared behind the same pillar she appeared from. Tim took a deep breath to compose himself and then sat back in his chair and relaxed.

"Wow, you two really don't like each other, do you?" asked Balthy.

"You can say that," replied Tim, as he picked up his latte and took a large sip. "We have a history and believe me when I say that she does not have your best interests at heart. Elley is only looking out for one person, and that is Elley. She is just like that questionable stain on your clothes that refuses to go away. But at least she is gone for now and I can enjoy my creamy beverage."

"I hear you, Tim. This has to be the best part of heaven, sitting around, talking with good friends about the secrets of life."

"Oh, it's not a secret Balthy," replied Tim, who had regained his composure and was now smiling happily across the table.

"It's not?"

"Nope! The secret is so simple that most people do not even realise it. I have seen some actors search for dozens of lifetimes searching for the answer to the secret and most usually give up without ever discovering it."

"Do you know what it is?"

"Of course I do! I'm an angel, remember? I was there when the very first script was written! Would you like to take a guess?"

Balthazar smiled and said, "Sure. Why not? Hmmm.....is it an Apple Martini or Cinnamon Squirrel?"

Tim laughed, "That is my secret of life! But what is yours?"

"That's a good question. What do I believe the secret of life is? Well, I can tell you what it is not. It's not a material thing because you can have everything you can ever want, only to have it taken away in the blink of an eye. How you react to that would be a secret of internal strength."

Across the table, Tim was staring intently as he listened.

"So, if it not material," continued Balthazar, "It would have to be something else, something possible for everyone to attain. It would have to be something simple that everyone overlooks."

"Go on," said Tim.

"Well, I may be completely off base here, but I believe the secret of life is happiness. The small things in life are what is most important, whether it is sharing a beautiful sunset with the person you love or enjoying a piece of quiche with a delicious cappuccino. Of course, I have a history of misreading things."

Tim stared in shock at Balthazar, his mouth agape as he tilted his head to the side and whispered, "You are absolutely right."

Balthy felt a shiver race down his spine and said, "I am?"

"Yes, you are! The secret of life is happiness. I have never seen anyone as young as you figure that out before. Never. You really are something special. I hope your next role will be worthy of your insights and talent."

"Thanks Tim, I appreciate the compliment. I would really like the chance to experience everything life has to offer; love, a family and a dream job, maybe as a fire-fighter. I think it would be so fun to slide down those poles."

Tim nodded and replied, "That does sound like fun."

As if on cue, a thick stack of tightly bound paper appeared on the table in front of Balthazar. He moved it closer and gently touched the embossed writing that glowed gold in the light. He smiled at Tim and turned to the first page of *The Bum*.

THE BUM

All he had was the watch she had given him; only that circular piecc of golden metal and nothing more.

The weather had been turning colder and the burning colour of the trees lining the street gave a warm welcome to what was to come. An icy blast whipped through the alley and cut easily through the scraps of filth wrapped around his emaciated form. A deep shiver convulsed through him as he slowly reached up and pulled his only protection from the elements tightly around him.

He wasn't much to look at now, time and the street had been hard on him. Greasy, unkempt hair fell limply from under a woollen cap and framed a face that was more skeletal than alive. Coarse, white stubble erupted from his leathery face and eyes that once were as green and bright as summer grassland in Ireland now were dull and milky, as his sight was slowly stolen by the oncoming darkness.

The streetlights hummed with an insolent glow that barely illuminated a single patch of light in his world of perpetual twilight. Pale, grey, concrete sidewalks snaked throughout the city like vericous veins, silent to all they had witnessed throughout the years.

He shuffled slowly toward the corner of a nearby building and gently eased himself down onto a heating grate. It wasn't much, but at least the periodic wafts of warm air would give him a momentary break from the cold.

Warmly dressed people shuffled quickly by and pretended not to notice him. He watched them intently and whenever a person caught his eye, they would stiffen and immediately look away. Women would clutch their purses so tightly when they saw him that their fingertips would turn as white and cold as the diamonds they wore.

He bore them no hard feelings; it was simply human nature.

Before everything that had happened, he had acted in the same manner. He would cringe inwardly whenever he saw a bum on the street because he knew that they would ask him for money; his money. He never understood why they simply did not get a job and make their own money instead. He had once even offered a guy minimum wage to carry his bags around for an hour. The person seemed insulted and he did not know why. That offer seemed more than fair. After all, he had worked very hard for his money, so why should he give it away? He thought the person would probably just use it to buy drugs or alcohol.

He discovered first hand that indeed, narcotics and liquor were the predominant amusement of choice amongst the street crowd. However, there were also people that did buy food with the donations.

There was a family of four living out of the back of their car behind one of the abandoned buildings where he stayed at night. Jim had been a factory worker and Gina had been a homemaker, responsible for taking care of their two young girls, Carlee and Brooke. In typical middle American fashion, they had been leveraged to the hilt with a large house and SUV they could not afford. They had barely been able to meet all their obligations, so when the plant unexpectedly closed, the bills quickly piled up and they lost everything.

Everyday Jim would be up at the crack of dawn and out in the city to look for work. He would do odd jobs whenever he could to try and earn enough money to put a bit of food into the stomachs of his family at night. On several occasions he had watched as both Jim and Gina would go hungry so Carlee and Brooke didn't have to.

It had been a long time since he had been impressed by anyone, but these were truly good people that were trying to make the best out of a horrible situation. Several months before it had been Brooke's fifth birthday and they had somehow managed to scratch together enough money to make her a tiny birthday cake. It was barely big enough to fit into the palm of his hand, but when the solitary candle was lit, he could tell from bright smile on Brooke's face that it was the best party in the world.

Her gift was a bar of chocolate, wrapped in the left over scraps of gold paper and tied with a soiled red ribbon. Her little face glowed with excitement at the sight of the sweet delight, but she did not tear into it. Instead she placed it on the tailgate, then carefully smoothed out the gold paper and gave it back to her mother.

Brooke must have noticed him staring at her from the shadows because she picked up her chocolate bar and walked over to him.

"Excuse me, mister," she said, looking at him with big, blue eyes, "Why do you look so sad?"

The question caught him so off guard that he stammered, "It's a very long story, little one."

"Is it because you are all alone?" asked Brooke.

"It is something like that. I miss someone very much."

Brooke looked at him for a moment, then nodded her head in understanding and extended her tiny hand. "My name is Brooke. What is yours?"

His name? It had been a long time since someone had asked that and it took a while to register. He looked nervously toward Jim and Gina who were watching intently and then gently reached out and engulfed her hand with his own and said, "It is a pleasure to meet you Brooke. My name is Brad."

They shook hands and Brooke said, "Hello Brad. Now we can be friends so you do not have to be alone anymore."

He felt his eyes begin to burn.

"It's my birthday. I'm five years old today. Would you like some of my chocolate bar?"

"No thanks, Brooke," he said in a voice that began to crack, "You enjoy it."

"O.K. Brad. I have to go back home now. Bye."

Brooke waived and then ran back to her parents who were staring in amazement at what had just transpired.

It had been an unexpected surprise talking with her.

No one talked to him.

Ever.

But that one little girl seemed to see something that no one else wanted to.

Just like Michelle.

He shifted his weight to relieve the pressure of the hard metal pressing into his hip and took a deep breath. Immediately he wished he hadn't as a coughing fit shook his skeletal form. His face turned scarlet and a large vein appeared in the middle of his forehead as he covered his mouth with his hand.

Several people looked on with disgust and decided to walk on the street rather than take the chance of coming into contact with such a pile of filth.

Soon the coughing subsided and the gurgling in his lungs became almost inaudible. He took his hand away from his mouth and was about to wipe the tears from his face when he saw flecks of moist, dark matter on the palm of his hand.

Blood.

That wasn't good.

There was not a lot he could do about it; it came with the territory. Too many years of being a smoke-eater; of inhaling every putrid concoction of man-made combustion. Of course he had used a respirator, but that only helped to a point, and only if he did not have to share his oxygen with somebody trapped in a structure. It was the life he had chosen and he did not regret it. He got to use an axe and ride in a big truck that came equipped with wailing sirens.

He always liked the sirens.

He had stopped by a free clinic when it had first happened and was met by an unpleasant nurse and indifferent doctor. They didn't care about his past or who he was as a person. To them, he was merely a number; a statistic variable that was input into a computer so they could get paid for seeing him.

The doctor had looked with disinterest over his test results and stated in a bored tone that unless he took a plethora of expensive antibiotics to help slow down the spread of the sickness, he would be dead within six months.

The news hit him like a blow to the chest and he went numb. He had seen death before, in his profession it had been unavoidable, but this was somehow different. For years he had longed for the sweet release of death, to leave all of this life's hardships behind and finally attain the peace that had been denied him since Michelle had went away. It had always been an abstract concept, something that happened to others, not him. Yet there he was, confronted by his own mortality inside a dingy building by a disillusioned practitioner of medicine.

When he told the doctor that he didn't have enough money for the drugs, the physician shrugged and said, "That's too bad. Such a waste of life. Talk to the Reverend on your way out."

While he could not say for certain, he could have sworn that he heard one of the nurses mumble something about one less gutter rat to worry about next year.

Most people would have been shattered to realise that they could be cured if they had the necessary monetary resources at their disposal, but not him. He found it strangely humorous that a few pieces of paper could extend his suffering by years, perhaps even decades. No. He had always met whatever life had to throw at him head on and had never backed away. Never. Not even when....when....

His mind rebelled against his attempt to think of her and another coughing fit wracked his frame, filling his mouth with the taste of copper. It hurt, but the pain reminded him he was still alive and she was worth remembering.

How long had it been? He closed his eyes and tried to think, but his mind felt heavy, like it was wrapped in lead. Long days and endless nights on the streets merged together to form a nightmare without end. But he fought through the mists clouding his thoughts and forced himself to remember her.

Michelle.

It must be going on six or seven years since she had been ripped away, since he had lost everything important to him. He missed her smile and the way she laughed at the little things in life. There had been times when he did not understand what was so funny, but her eyes would gleam mischievously and she would tell him that it was always the little things that mattered the most.

It was amazing how things worked out because their first meeting had been less than spectacular.

They had met on a blind date during the summer of his University graduation when he had been working as a waiter at a resort near where she lived. She had just broken up with a long term boyfriend and he had been funnelling beer through a pink garden flamingo all night, so the meeting was interesting to say the least.

He remembered that she sat with her legs tightly crossed, foot twitching like a cat's tail as she took heavy drags on her cigarette and stared blankly off into space as he was rambling on about something from his childhood.

He paused and said, "I don't know why I am telling you this."

Michelle stared coldly back at him and replied, "Neither do I."

He ignored her and continued prattling on because he was drunk and didn't care about the nasty comment she made, after all, it was not like he would ever talk to her again after that night.

He was wrong.

Years passed by and then he made the trip north to attend his friends wedding and meet his mystery date.

It was Michelle.

The Fates obviously had a sense of humour.

His parents had always taught him to be polite, and always hold himself as a gentleman. But when he saw those familiar locks of golden hair, he knew that he had his work cut out for him.

He took a deep breath, gave her his best smile, extended his hand and introduced himself. He could tell from the look on her face that she remembered him all too well, but she smiled and allowed her hand to disappear into his.

Then something strange happened. They started to talk and the entire night disappeared in an instant.

They continued to talk every night for hours and before he could blink, years had passed and she had become part of his wholeness and he hers. They talked about everything; their thoughts, dreams, hopes for the future and even what heaven might be like.

She believed that life was an adventure and when we died, we simply went to a place where we were most happy.

He figured out a long time ago that our life was a journey that had both a set departure and arrival point, just like an aeroplane. The aeroplane represents the outer shell, or body of the traveller and helps them get from point to point, while the passengers inside the plane represent the spirit, or soul. We occupy space inside the vehicle for a set length of trip, and when it is over, we simply exit the vessel and begin another journey. We travel with many others, but our journey remains our own.

She had nodded in understanding and then suggested that he cut down on his recreational drug use.

They were married in October and it was then that she had surprised him with an unexpected gift; a golden pocket watch. He could still remember the mischievous glint in her eyes when she handed him the tiny gift. The back was inscribed with their secret names and inside the cover was a picture from the night they had met again at their friend's wedding.

"I don't know what to say," he had told her as he rolled the watch around between his sausage-like fingers.

"Just say that you'll keep it safe," she had replied.

"I will," he whispered, "I just wish there was something I could give you."

Michelle smiled slyly and purred as she reached for the light, "I'm sure I can think of something."

Soon after she became pregnant and would spend hours staring at herself in the mirror, gently touching where a new life was growing inside of her. All of his friends told him not to worry because they would find the bastard responsible for knocking her up. They hoped it was a boy because that way he only had to worry about one penis, whereas if it was a girl, he would have to worry about an entire town of penises. He remembered laughing until the wisdom behind the words sunk in. Yep, he hoped it was a boy!

Time seemed to fly by and it wasn't long before she had developed a little bump and was devouring everything in the fridge. He had heard of pregnant women getting cravings for odd combinations of food, but when Michelle added pickles and french fries to fruit yogurt, he had to rub his eyes to ensure he was not seeing things.

Then things changed.

Forever.

He remembered every little thing as if it happened only yesterday. The air was crisp and cold and the ground was slippery because of an ice storm they had earlier that day. A thin layer of white snow framed the branches of the trees outside their home and the sky was bright with a full moon.

They had gone to the doctor's office for her check-up and had declined when he asked them if they wanted to know the gender of the baby. They originally wanted to be surprised, but by the time they got home, they could not wait anymore. They immediately placed a call back to the doctor and had been waiting by the phone for the response to their question.

He had to leave for work, so he put on his leather coat, leaned down and gave her a quick kiss goodbye and said, "Call me when you know it's a boy."

"You know it's going to be a little girl, right?" replied Michelle.

He hung his head in defeat and muttered, "Yeah, you are probably right. It's my own fault; I shouldn't have gone so deep."

Michelle laughed and patted his arm.

"I'm going to bed soon, so if I can't get hold of you I will leave a message on the table for you."

He nodded and flashed her a bright smile as he opened the door.

"Be careful," she said.

"I always am. After all, I'm not that easy to get rid of! Especially with my good luck charm," he replied, patting the watch inside his coat.

He winked at her and closed the door.

If only he had known that was the last time they would talk, he would have told her that he loved her. If he had taken the night off work.....if only.....

He shook his head and swallowed hard. It served no purpose thinking about what might have been because it didn't happen. The last image he had of Michelle was her sitting on the couch with the phone beside her, nervously picking at her nails.

The door closed and he remembered the snow crunching under his boots and how cold the door handle felt on his fingertips. His favourite Meatloaf song was playing on the radio and he had turned it up and sang along all the way to the station.

He remembered the night was slow and it seemed to drag by as he waited and waited for her call that never came.

By early morning he was already planning what he was going to do to Michelle when he got home for not phoning him with the news. Perhaps ice-cold hands on her warm back....yes...that was a great idea. He was lost in thought of his evilness when the fire alarm went off, shattering his train of thought.

Years of training took over as he leapt out of the comfort of the chair, down the pole and over to his locker in seconds. He was fully dressed and almost at the truck when the dispatcher read the address over the speakers.

Everything moved into slow motion. He looked at his buddies because he thought he misheard the information, but he knew from the looks on their faces, he hadn't.

The address was his.

Michelle.

The fire station's doors whipped upward and the engine roared into pristine whiteness, its sirens splitting the serenity of the night with a piercing wail. The few cars out on the road quickly pulled to the side and let the streaking red bullet pass.

They arrived at his street within a few minutes of the call, but by then his home was completely engulfed in flame. Thick plumes of black smoke spiralled upward, beckoned on by the tongues of orange and red flame that licked at their base.

He grabbed his axe and ran toward the front of the house, leaving his respirator, gloves and helmet behind. He had to get to her; get her out of the house before it was too late. He reached the door and instead of checking it for potential danger, brought the axe down with all his might.

All he remembered was the suction of air rushing into the house and then nothing but flame. The explosive force of the back draft hit him like a train and blew him backward over twenty feet into the thick trunk of a tree. He heard the wet snap of several ribs and then everything went black.

He woke up in the hospital several weeks later.

Michelle never did.

He was told that they found her curled up in bed, smiling with a note clutched in her hand with his name on it. They tried to resuscitate her, but it was too late for her and the baby. It was a small blessing that the fire never got to her; it was the smoke that ensured she never woke from her peaceful dreams.

They gave him the note on which was written, "You just have to worry about one penis.....:)"

He roared and remembered nothing more.

The fire Marshall investigated the cause of the blaze and determined it had been deliberately set. Witnesses reported seeing a slight figure, probably a woman, with deep red hair running from the scene minutes before flame engulfed the building, but the police had no leads and it was likely they never would.

His world cracked and fell apart.

He sold all he owned and just walked away from everybody and everything that reminded him of her. He became one of the lost, blending in seamlessly with the disillusioned of the world. The emptiness of the city embraced him like a lost child and welcomed his hollowness as a kindred spirit.

Weeks became months that became years. Now he was a nobody. After all, when was the last time a person like him ever help change the world or influence an outcome? Never. It was just the way things were.

He couldn't save her - save them. He could not even save himself.

Now here he was, sitting on a heating grate, absently stroking his golden treasure, remembering things he had no business thinking about.

He scratched the white stubble on his chin and sighed. It didn't matter now; nothing did. Soon the pain of this life would be over one way or another. There were many times during those first few months alone that he considered ending everything; to crawl gracelessly into the darkness.

He wasn't sure anymore about what happened after we died, and to be honest, he didn't really care. All he knew was that a piece of him had been ripped away and pain was all that remained behind.

He had it all planned. The note had been written, the hot bath drawn and the instrument of his end was between his fingertips. He remembered thinking, straight up the forearm, when he caught a whiff of a familiar perfume. For just the briefest of moments he swore that he saw Michelle's face in the bathroom mirror and then she was gone.

To this day, he wasn't sure if it was Michelle or just his mind's way of ensuring its self preservation. To be honest, he didn't really care. He would like to think that she had better things to do with her time than hang out in bathrooms, watching him bathe in the nude. That being said, if he were a ghost, he would probably hang around in the women's showers at the gym just for the heck of it.

Another icy blast whipped across him and brought him crashing back to reality. It was early evening and the crowds had thinned out considerably. They had gone to their homes and he should do the same before it got too dark.

He didn't like being out in the open when it got dark. As the sun retreated, the scum of society emerged from the crevices of the city like cockroaches, ready to feast on everything in their path. Many years before he remembered reading about the murder of a child prostitute in a nearby alleyway. He had been very young, but there was something about the two coins found beside her that made it stick in his memory.

This city was a mere shade of what it once was. Years of mismanagement and corruption had gutted the gleam and left behind only festering ugliness. If any type of disaster were to strike this place, it would be considered urban renewal. Yeah, that was just what this place deserved, a good cleansing by fire.

It always took away everything.

With great difficulty he hoisted himself to his feet and shuffled back down the maze of alleyways toward the box that he called home. It wasn't much to look at, but after he insulated it with old egg cartons and newspapers, it was definitely warmer than outside.

He could see his breath and the parts of his body that had been pressed against the heating grate were slightly less numb than the other extremities. He had always thought that the worst part about being out on the street would be hunger, but he was wrong. He quickly discovered that it was warmth; or lack thereof. The hunger he could deal with, but not having the ability to drink something warm was the worst part. How he missed the simple pleasure of plugging in the kettle for a hot cup of tea. Yes, a hot cup of tea was his favourite thing.

Oh well. There was nothing he could do about it now. All he had to look forward to was another restless night on the unforgiving ground. It could be worse, at least he did not have a family to look after.

That reminded him, he wondered how Jim was getting on at his new job. He had just started working for a company that cleaned out old buildings to get them ready for demolition. The job was permanent and Jim was working as many hours as he could to try and save enough money to get his family off the street. He had been working at a jobsite near the empty lot, so he was able to work sixteen hour days and still spend time with Gina, Carlee and Brooke on his breaks.

The family seemed happier than they had been in a very long time, and ever since Brooke's birthday party, they had adopted him as a sort of uncle figure. For some strange reason, Brooke liked him and he did not know why.

Wow, that little girl could talk!

She would wander over to his box and just start talking relentlessly about anything and everything. She never stopped. It didn't matter the time or day or the weather outside, as soon as she caught sight of him, the chattering would start. He hated people at the best of times, but here was a little girl who ignored all his protests and latched onto him like a moray eel.

After a few weeks of this constant torment, he gave up and accepted his Fate. As long as the family remained in their car, he would never get his peace and quiet, so had to make the best out of the situation.

Soon he could see the end of the alley and pressed against the slimy wall was what passed as his home. He moved up to the opening of his box and braced himself for the flurry of excited questions that Brooke would have for him.

Nothing happened.

The quiet caught him off guard and he scanned the lot, searching for the bouncing ball of blond hair. There was the vehicle with Carlee in the backseat and Gina in the front, but Brooke was nowhere to be found.

That was strange.

He emerged stiffly from the alleyway and as he was about to shout to Gina, his nose caught an all too familiar smell on the crisp night air.

Smoke.

It was close.

Very close.

Gina must have smelt the same thing because she jumped out of the car and froze in her tracks. He followed her line of sight and saw thin columns of white smoke escaping from the roof of a nearby warehouse.

He knew from the expression on her face that the burning building was where Jim was working, but he had to be sure.

"Gina!" he shouted, "Where is Jim? Where's Brooke?"

Gina heard his voice and turned to face him. All the blood had drained from her face and her eyes were wide and glazed in fright.

She stammered, "He's working in that building. Brooke is with him. She wanted to surprise him with some dinner, so I let her bring it to him. But she's not back. I never thought...."

He reached out and grabbed her shoulder gently and gave it a reassuring squeeze. "I'm sure there is nothing to worry about," he said in a calm voice, "But I will go and check for you, to make sure there are no problems."

She sniffed and wiped her eyes, never taking them from the building.

"But I need you to do something for me. Find a phone and call 9-1-1. Let them know that the building is on fire and where it is located. Can you do that?"

Gina shook her head and he immediately turned and limped toward the building. He forced his eyes to focus on his destination, to scan the base of the building for any signs of life.

There were none.

He watched the slivers of white smoke thicken and darken as they rose from the building. That wasn't good. As he drew closer, he could see the first tongues of flame snaking outward, licking the heavy roof beams and running along their dry forms. That was the problem with this type of old warehouse; they were so dry and full of waste product, that they were a tinderbox waiting to go up with the introduction of a single spark.

Now he could hear the crackling of the beast that had cost him everything in life. He could sense it growing, feeding, and becoming stronger and brighter with every passing second. It knew he was close and it wanted to embrace him.

It wouldn't be long before the entire structure was engulfed and unless the boys got there soon, they might lose the entire block.

He moved to the front of the building and stopped by the front door. It was ajar and thick, black smoke poured out of it and up the brickwork. He tried peering through the smoke to see if anyone was inside, but he could not see a thing.

Fear knotted his stomach and he felt physically ill as he stared into the burning abyss of his past. Every sensation, every thought, every emotion came rushing back, overwhelming his senses and making his head spin. He had tried for years to forget who he was, to forget what had happened, but now it appeared he couldn't. No one could escape their past.

A cloud of smoke insolently enveloped his face and burrowed into his lungs, causing a coughing fit to wrack his frail form. There was the familiar taste of copper and something else; something he had forgotten about, something he missed.

He was a smoke eater; always had been, always will be. He realised that now. Maybe in a few days he would try and contact the guys at the old hall and see how he could become involved again. He owed that to himself. He owed that to her.

He took a step back and waited to hear the sound of the sirens. He could see no sign that anyone was inside. Jim and Brooke were not there, they couldn't be. He probably took her out for an ice cream before this even happened.

Strange, he felt relieved about that. What did that little girl do to him?

He turned and was about to walk away when a high pitched scream stopped him in his tracks. He felt his stomach drop to his ankles.

Oh no. Brooke.

What was going to do? Or to be more specific, what could he do? He took a step toward the door and stopped. Who was he trying to fool? Too many years had passed and he had allowed his body to become what it was now. He had no strength left, his joints were so stiff that he could barely walk and he could barely breathe. If he tried to help, he would need rescuing as well.

No. He would wait for the boys to arrive and let them handle the situation. That would be for the best. He closed his eyes and strained his hearing to pick up on expected sound of a siren. Still he heard nothing but the crackling of the fire and the popping of windows as the flames searched out a new source of oxygen.

Brooke screamed again, but it was cut off by a coughing fit.

Then he remembered that fires rarely kill people, the smoke does the job instead. His head flicked around, searching for somebody to help him, but the space was empty. He was by himself.

Indecision raced through his mind, he didn't know what to do. Part of him wanted to simply turn and walk away; to leave the people inside to their fate. It wasn't his problem. He didn't care.

But the other part of him, the part buried deep inside, screamed at him to do something. Brooke was just a little girl that deserved every chance life had to offer her; she shouldn't have her adventures cut short because a decrepit, old bum decided to do nothing. She offered him some of her birthday chocolate and talked to him when no one else would.

He couldn't let anything happen to her. He wouldn't.

He reached down and patted the golden circle, his good luck charm, threw his shoulders back and went through the doorway.

A deep veil of smoke enveloped his body and he could feel the intense heat as he dropped to his hands and knees in an attempt to get under the cloud of black death. His only chance was to crawl along the floor, using the walls as a guide to search each room for Jim and Brooke. He paused to wrap one of his filthy rags around his nose and mouth and then continued moving in a set pattern from the doorway.

His training came back to him as he kept a mental map of where he searched, using the base of the first wall as guide post.

Time had no meaning here. It had always amazed him how time ceased to exist in an environment where it should mean the most. It was a conundrum that did not escape him because the longer he took to find them, the more chance there was that they would not survive.

Suddenly his outstretched fingers touched something soft and warm. It was an arm; Jim's arm. He moved forward and located his head to check for any sign of life. Luck seemed to be with him because Jim was still breathing, though barely. The smoke had already started to do its work.

He did a quick check of Jim's extremities to make sure that nothing was missing and then dragged him toward the nearby door. He was heavier than he looked and though it was extremely difficult to manipulate his body out the door, he managed to do it.

Jim started coughing as soon as the outside air washed over him and had regained a measure of consciousness by the time they had reached a safe distance from the building.

Jim's eyes were darting back and forth without focusing on anything and he could tell from the leg that was bent backward at a bizarre angle, the pain must have been intense.

His eyes were burning, his lungs felt as though they were made of metal and it seemed as though a giant hand was crushing his chest. He knew his body was in a bad way, but he couldn't stop now. Brooke needed him.

"Jim!" he screamed. "Jim! Can you hear me?"

Jim blinked and tried to figure out who was talking to him.

"Up here! Jim, I need to know, where is Brooke?"

Jim's body convulsed in a coughing fit and he managed to wheeze, "Back left room....went to get the fire extinguisher.....couldn't get to her in time....tried...fell..."

Jim's eyes rolled back in his head as unconsciousness took him again.

In the distance he could hear a solitary siren, then two and soon an entire chorus of wailing sirens intermingled with blasts from an air horn to warn people to get out of the way.

He felt that familiar jolt of excitement surge up his spine and he knew that they would be there soon.

But not soon enough.

He heard a crack followed by a loud explosion as a portion of the roof collapsed inward, sending bright orange cinders whirling skyward against a background of black smoke. He had always found it strangely beautiful, but now it merely reminded him that the fire was not happy at losing one of its victims and it was going to make sure it would not lose another.

He hauled himself to his feet and went back to the doorway used to be. Both doors had been blown outward and several pieces of burning wood blocked the entrance. Much of the smoke had disappeared up the hole where the roof used to be, which allowed him a rare, unfettered glimpse into the core of the building.

What greeted his eyes resembled something from Dante's Inferno. Different colours of flame were everywhere, greedily engulfing everything it came into contact with. Debris littered the floor and he could feel the intense heat blistering his skin. Nothing could survive in there for long. He would have to move quickly.

He had nothing to chop through the burning pieces of wood blocking the doorway, so he improvised and used his shoulder to force his way into the structure. The pieces gave way so easily that he stumbled and fell on top of one of them.

He rolled off it and cursed at himself for being so stupid. It was a rookie mistake and he was far too old to be making those. He angrily brushed himself off and paused at his right side. It was wet.

He felt no pain, so it couldn't be that bad. He ignored it and looked toward the back left corner of the room where Jim said Brooke disappeared to. He brought his hand up to try and shield his face from the heat and caught a glimpse of blonde hair buried under some rubble.

There was a clear path toward her position and he was able to get there in a matter of seconds. What he saw made the squeezing in his chest intensify. There was Brooke, buried waist deep in ceiling debris with a burning cross member laying across her, pinning her beneath its flame.

Her eyes were closed and a fire extinguisher that was almost as large as she was rested beside her closed hand. Her hair lay in a golden ring around her head like a halo and her soot covered face looked as though she were sleeping.

No. Not like this. She doesn't deserve this. She's just a little girl. This can't happen. I won't allow this to happen!

He used his hands as shovels and did his best to remove the pile of debris covering her tiny form. His hands must be cut, but he did not feel it. He didn't even feel the sweltering heat from the giant wooden timber anymore. He was immune to all pain except the one in his chest.

In no time he had cleared everything that was covering Brooke and breathed a huge sigh of relief when he saw her chest move up and down.

"Brooke? Brooke, can you hear me, sweetie?" he said, gently touching her face.

Brooke stirred and slowly opened her eyes.

"Good! That's good! Say something."

Her eyes focused on him and she said, "I knew you would come. Where's daddy?"

"He's outside, waiting just for you."

"I tried to help with the fire extinguisher, but I couldn't move it; it was too big"

"You are such a brave little girl! Now we have to get you out of here. Are you ready to leave?"

She shook her head and picked nervously at her fingernails.

"OK, good. I need to know if you are hurt. Does it hurt anywhere? Can you move your legs?"

Brooke stuck out her bottom lip in concentration and said, "No, I'm fine. I just can't get up because my legs are trapped under this piece of wood. Stupid wood."

He quickly surveyed the scene and saw that the giant piece of burning timber was laying across her legs, pinning her to the floor. While not all of the support piece was on fire, it was spreading quickly and would be entirely engulfed within a matter of minutes.

He didn't know what to do. The piece of wood had to weigh at least a thousand pounds and he had no way of manuvering it off her. If he had a chainsaw or axe, he could cut through it. If he had an airbag, he could inflate it enough to pull her out, but he did not have anything.

To make matters worse, he could hear the cracking of the remaining support beams and he knew the entire structure could collapse at any moment. If he waited for the others, they were both dead, either from the flame or from the building collapsing on them. The pain in his chest had spread to his arm and he could hear himself wheezing. He was out of time.

He knew what he had to do.

He smoothed Brooke's hair away from her face and said, "I need you to be brave one more time. Can you do that?"

Brooke nodded her head and he continued, "Good girl. I'm going to try and lift this piece of wood off you, and as soon as you can get your legs free, I want you to run as fast as you can toward the doorway. Don't look back, just keep running until you see your dad."

"What about you?"

He smiled, reached into his front pocket and pulled out his watch.

"See this?" he asked, "This is my lucky charm. It was given to me by a very special person and it means more than anything to me. I want you to hold onto it for me until I come back for it. That way you know that I will be fine."

He pressed the golden circle into her hand and she closed her fingers tightly around it.

"Are you ready?"

He looked at the flames running up the wood and realised there was no where to lift that wasn't burning. Then he looked at Brooke's face, so trusting, so innocent. He couldn't let the flames ruin her the way they had ruined him.

He girded himself against the certain pain, bent down, grabbed the burning wood and lifted. Nothing happened. He held his breath and tried again. Still nothing. He could smell something burning and realised it was him, but he felt no pain. Everything seemed to be getting farther away, even the pain in his chest and arm was not as bad as it had been.

"Come on!" he screamed to himself, "Lift it!"

He clenched his teeth together and tried one last time with everything he had left.

He smelled cinnamon.

The timber began to move.

His muscles flexed to their limit and beyond; his ligaments tore, but still he lifted that flaming crossbeam upward until it was off the little girl.

He held it long enough for Brooke to make it to the doorway, and just as she went through, the building collapsed around him.

ACT SIX

The glow from the flames faded away as did the crippling pain in his chest. He knew instinctually that this was the end, his time on Earth was through, and he was fine with that.

It was a fair trade.

The life of an innocent little girl in exchange for a decrepit, old bum that no one would miss. He had squandered his chance at making a difference, but hopefully Brooke would not make the same mistake.

The wail of sirens grew louder and more distant at the same time. He tried to blink, but found his eyes were fixed on the night sky through the collapsed roof. It was a beautiful night and the stars shone brighter than he had ever seen before. One bright patch of light twinkled and seemed to grow more and more brilliant with every passing second until it enveloped his broken form. He felt himself being drawn upward at incredible speed and suddenly there was a flash and he found himself standing at the entrance of a building.

Close by he heard a strangely familiar voice say, "Marky, I need your opinion. Do these wings make me look fat?"

Brad tentatively stepped foot into the golden, wooden structure and turned his head toward where the voice came from. Nearby he saw two immaculately dressed people standing in front of a full length mirror. One had long ringlets of flaming red hair and was wearing solid black, while the other had short, spiky, fluorescent blond hair and was wearing a shiny, hunter green coloured dress shirt and crisp white slacks. The strange part was both of the people had large, feathery wings on their back that did not interfere with the lines of their shirts.

They had to be angels.

"Of course we are angels," said the one in black, "Were you expecting trumpets and ill fitting robes?"

"Be nice Marcus," replied the angel in hunter green as he turned around to admire his wings from behind, "I don't have time to fight right now because I'm expecting someone shortly and I want to look good."

"Please! Tim, you know that we always look good," said Marcus.

"You're right, as usual. Go have yourself an apple martini and I will catch up with you later and we can discuss the party," replied Tim, straightening the pleat on the sleeve of his shirt.

Marcus nodded his head toward Brad and then disappeared into thin air. Tim looked up from his mirror and smiled warmly.

"Oh, hello there Balthy!" said Tim, waving excitedly to him. "You're just in time to help me with an important decision. See, I've decided to throw a spectacular party, everyone will be there, and I can't decide what to wear. I mean, I already *know* what I'll wear, after all, things are much more conservative now compared to the Bacchus parties the ancient Greeks used to put on! I'm telling you, there was so much naked flesh everywhere that I was actually speechless."

"What are you talking about? Who are you?" asked Brad in a confused voice.

"That's right! I forgot that you just got back and are probably a bit confused. Here, have a seat," said Tim, pulling an oversized, stuffed chair away from the table, ""I'm Tim and I'll be right back with a hot Latte and a piece of my delicious quiche. It truly is a sinful delight!"

Brad shook his head and slowly eased himself into the chair. He rubbed his eyes to make sure that he wasn't seeing things, but the cafe and tables filled with people didn't disappear. The place seemed both enormous and quaint at the same time, it was unlike anything he had ever experienced before. Yet, it felt familiar, like the shadow of a memory of a dream. He knew this place, but couldn't remember how. Maybe he was imagining all this. He could be lying in a hospital bed, hooked up to machines and in deep coma.

"No, I'm afraid that you are not dreaming," said Tim, appearing out of nowhere with two cups of steaming Latte and a slice of beautifully cooked quiche.

"That means that I'm,"

"Dead," interrupted Tim as he took a small sip of his drink, "That's right. You got squished flatter than my pastry dough."

The news should have hit him hard, but he found that he was strangely neutral about the news. He was more concerned for the safety of Brooke and said, "What about the little girl? Did she make out alright?"

Tim smiled, leaned forward and replied, "Yes, thanks to you, she will be fine."

Brad breathed a huge sigh of relief and picked up the deep mug for a drink.

"And I must say," continued Tim, "What you did down there was spectacular! I got such a chill down my spine when you reached down, grabbed that burning timber with your bare hands and pulled it off that little girl! Oh, I was crying for hours! That wasn't in the script, but that impromptu performance was amazing. And the part about worrying about an entire city of penises was priceless - I haven't laughed so hard since Augustus showed up wearing stripes and plaid together in one outfit. I mean, pick one thing and stay with it! What was he thinking?"

"You saw me? Saw us?" questioned Brad, "Saw *everything?*"

Tim smirked and he said, "Indeed, and I must compliment you on your athleticism - it is very deceiving."

Brad felt his face turning red and he was about to say something crude when he remembered about Michelle. He looked at Tim and asked, "I'm in heaven, right?"

"You are."

"Then where is Michelle? Is she nearby? I have to see her."

Tim took a deep breath and replied sadly, "I'm sorry Balthy, she is not here."

"What do you mean she's not here? She has to be!" said Brad, raising his voice, "She was a good person - much better than I was! How can I be here without her?"

"It's not that simple Balthy," said Tim softly, reaching out a perfectly manicured hand to pat him on the forearm, "She already took another role and is back on Earth."

"Another role? What are you talking about? And why do you keep calling me Balthy? My name is Brad."

"Of course it is. Take a sip of your Latte and you will understand everything, trust me. After all, is this a face that would lie to you?" Tim tilted his porcelain-like face upward and he could swear that he heard angelic singing in the background - which is exactly what it was. They were practising for the upcoming party and just happened to have exquisite timing.

Brad looked suspiciously at Tim and then took a tiny sip.

As soon as the delicious liquid touched his tongue, he felt a surge of memory rush through him. No longer did he feel lost as when he would wake up from a dream and try to remember what it was. Everything he had chosen to forget when he was born came roaring back in great detail.

He remembered everything.

He was both Brad *and* Balthazar. They were one in the same person, and sitting across from him was the angel who he had befriended so long ago.

"Hello again, Tim," said Bal, "I see you've decided to go blond - it looks really good."

Tim smiled and subconsciously rang his fingers through his hair.

"Do you really like it?" asked Tim.

Bal nodded in agreement.

"Why thank you! You're sweet. Somedays it takes me hours to get it right and I get so flustered that I want to shave it all off, right to the scalp! But then I remember that beauty takes time and no angel looks good with a bald head. But enough about me! Let's dish. Tell me all about your latest role as *The Bum*."

Bal stuck out his bottom lip in thought and then took a bite of Tim's award winning quiche. He chewed thoughtfully and said, "This is the best quiche I have ever had! You have truly outdone yourself yet again, my friend. One of these days you are going to have to tell me your secret."

Tim squirmed happily on his seat and blushed, but did not say anything.

"Well," continued Bal, "I can honestly say that even though I read what was going to happen, I was not expecting the ferocity of emotions associated with the loss of my wife and unborn child. It was really rough and I lost the plot, literally. That was the first time I wish he hadn't written free will into the story. I felt my world collapse and it was a heartache I never wish to experience again."

Tim's face softened and he nodded empathetically.

"I could have pulled myself back to my feet and continued doing the job I loved, but I just could not bring myself to slide down the pole any more."

"I can't imagine what that must be like," interjected Tim.

"And I hope you never have to," replied Bal. "Everything changed that night. I wanted to write myself out of the story, forever, and I would have if I didn't see her in the mirror. Was that her?"

Tim nodded.

"So she did show up to stop me. Hmmm," said Bal, stroking his chin, "I thought so, but wasn't entirely certain. Anyway, the rest of my life was full of anguish and suffering. Life on the street is incredibly hard and the way people react to you is strangely fascinating to observe first hand. Most people don't care about your story and aren't interested in trying to help; all they care about is money. Just once I would like to see a person with money make a difference to those around them. You don't even need money to make a difference; sometimes all that is necessary is a kind word,"

"Like Brooke on her birthday?" asked Tim.

Bal's eyes burned momentarily before he replied in a choked voice, "Exactly. That tiny gesture saved me."

They sat silently for a moment while Bal regained his composure and had another sip of Latte.

"Speaking of women," said Tim, breaking the silence, "You remember Cera, don't you? She is a truly gifted actress," said Tim.

"That's one way of putting it," replied Balthazar, "The only thing she is gifted at is making my life difficult. I don't know if I will ever be ready to share the stage with her."

Tim smiled and said, "You know, she said nearly the exact same thing about you the night that she came back."

"That doesn't surprise me."

Tim raised his hand to cut him off and said, "Let me finish. See, you've already worked together, and to great reviews I must say."

Then he understood.

Cera was Michelle.

"She said that you were one of the biggest pains she had ever experienced, but she respected your abilities and asked to work with you *again*."

Bal's jaw hung slack in amazement and for the first time in his life he didn't know what to say.

"I know! I was so shocked that I actually dropped a cup of hot chocolate on my magenta silk! It's incredibly creamy, but a lion to try and remove. But it gets better," said Tim, leaning across the table and lowering his voice. "You see, Cera wanted to work with you again so much that she turned down several key roles and waited until something came up with you in it."

"No way," said Bal.

"Way!" replied Tim, leaning back in his chair and crossing his legs, "Normally that never would have been allowed and she never would have worked again, but she caught the attention of the casting director and he was so impressed that he wrote something special for the both of you."

"I thought you said that she had already taken another role?" asked Bal.

"She has and it is in production as we speak."

"Then how is it that we would share the same story? Unless...Oh no."

Tim's smile broadened until it went from ear to ear.

Michelle was Brooke.

"She risked her career for me?" asked Bal, shaking his head in disbelief. "That doesn't make sense. She's truly the most frustrating woman I have ever met! She always has to be right, always has to get the last word in. She drives me crazy!"

Tim nodded and smiled slyly.

"You must have made quite the impression on her."

"As you have on us," said Elley, appearing out of thin air with a waft of cinnamon. "That last role was one of the most magnificent we have ever had the privilege of witnessing. You were so close to having it all: a loving wife, a child and the job of your dreams! Then it was all taken away from you in the blink of an eye and the flash of a match."

Bal felt an all too familiar stab of pain and he said, "What's your point?"

Elley smiled and said softly, "Just that nobody deserves to suffer like you did. I can't imagine the horror that you experienced during your last role. It must have been like a nightmare that you could not wake up from."

"That is exactly how I felt, and all my trouble began with some lady setting fire to my home. Why would someone do that?"

"Why indeed," said Tim, staring coldly at Elley.

"It must have been scripted that way," hissed Elley innocently, "But why would the head writer want you to suffer so much? What have you done to deserve that?"

"I'm not sure," whispered Balthazar, "But I've had so many hard roles that I really want to try something different. I want the family, career and full life that I have never experienced before. There is so much suffering in the world that I would give anything to change."

"Really?" asked Elley, her interest peaking, "You would be willing to give anything to make a change? Try anything for the dream?"

Balthazar took a deep breath and then exhaled loudly, "I would definitely try anything to help. Why do you ask?"

"Oh, no reason really," said Elley, a smile playing at the corners of her mouth. "It's just that my studio has put together a script of their own for you, and they were wondering if you would be interested in reading it."

"They would do that for me?" asked Balthazar.

"Not only would they do it for you, they have! Mr. Cypher believes in your ability so much that the studio put everything else on hold so you could get this role."

"But if I take a look at your script, does that mean that I have to sign with your studio?"

"Not at all. We just want to give you the opportunity of choice. Take a lifetime and see what you think of our work and if at the end of it, you don't want to work with us again, there is no hard feelings. You have nothing to lose."

"Be careful, Balthy," warned Tim as he glared at the smirking form of Elley, "There is always a catch."

Bal's face grew red and he stammered, "Well, if they has so much belief in me, I suppose it wouldn't hurt to see the script. Do you have it with you?"

"Hot off the presses," said Elley, "Here you go, Balthazar."
Elley reached under the table cloth and withdrew a thick, tightly bound stack of paper. It looked almost identical to the previous scripts he had read, except the binding was black and the raised lettering was red. She paused for a moment to admire the beautifully crafted lettering on the first page before placing it down in front of Balthazar.

Bal gently traced the raised letters with his finger and opened the pages of *The Businessman.*

THE BUSINESSMAN

Thump-thump. Thump-thump. Thump-thump.

He knew two things for sure; he was going to die and he still loved her as much today as he did when they first met over fifty years before.

How the hell did that happen?

"You look lost in thought," said Brooke softly as she gently brushed the matted hair back from his forehead.

He turned his head and looked at the woman who had shared so much of his life with, so very much of it, and replied, "I'm just remembering how lucky I am that we have been together for over fifty wonderful years. Yep, six hundred months; eighteen thousand days."

Brooke's eyes lit up as she smiled and said, "You're a bad liar."

She was good.

"You are probably thinking how the hell do you still love me after all that time."

She was very good.

"No," he stammered, "Not at all! I count my blessing every time I wake up and see that you didn't die during the night."

"Uh, huh."

"Seriously, would I lie to you with my health in such a bad way? That would be crazy! It's not like I take that phrase 'till death do us part' literally. I'm not looking forward to checking out the hotties on the other side, even though I will be a chick magnet."

"I hate to burst your bubble," laughed Brooke as she leaned forward, "But you are not going to get rid of me that easily. See, I waited a long time for you to show up and one lifetime is not enough."

"Yes it is. I'm sure of it."

"Good try, but it is not going to happen."

"Are you sure? I mean, I'd do this for you if you really wanted."

"Hmmm, let me think about that for a moment. No."

"Oh, come on!

Brooke shook her head and said, "No. I'm afraid you are stuck with me."

He stuck out his bottom lip and muttered, "Shit."

Thump-thump. Thump-thump. Thump-thump.

He could hear his heart beat; that was never a good sign. In fact he was hooked up to so many machines that if he were to pass gas, at least three of them would explode from information overload.

He hated hospitals. This was not some simple dislike brought about by lack of information, it was the real deal. He hated the lighting, the colour and the smell. Especially the smell.

All his life he had an almost wolf-like sense of smell. He could pick up on scents better than anyone he knew, but it came with a price. There had been times when the intensity of an odour made the room spin and him blow chunks.

One such experience that remained firmly in his mind was when he was in his early thirties and he had taken Brooke to the zoo. She had always wanted to go and he thought it could be worth some major points if he were the one to take her.

Everything went well and they saw many interesting animals including a yawning hippo, a friendly giraffe, a sleeping polar bear and an elephant that posed for pictures. Then they entered the African pavilion to see the gorillas.

His mistake.

The smell of the animals rushed up and hit him across the face like a brick bat. The humidity combined with the mixture of aromas to create something with a life unto itself. It wasn't just a single smell, rather it had so many distinct layers and not so subtle nuances that every breath was like an assault on his senses.

Anytime you combine the pungent body odour of the gorillas with urine and dung in a sauna-like environment, nothing good could come of it.

He could almost chew the stench, it was so thick. His stomach flipped over and over as it did its best to alleviate the nausea by eliminating the pizza he had for lunch. In the end he managed to get outside before he puked, but just barely. Now if ever he were on an African safari, he could identify the smell of Gorillas for their guide.

Hospitals were not much better. Everywhere smelled like cleaner, hand sanitizer, body waste and plastic. He hated this place so much that he had checked himself out a few weeks earlier to spend a few last days with his family.

The doctors and nurses had told him that he was not allowed to leave the hospital because of his condition. That lasted all of about two seconds before he informed the staff exactly what he was going to do with his cane if they tried to stop him. They had no legal ground to stand on and they knew it. For some reason, not many people realised that you could refuse any treatment you wish and you did not have to remain in the hospital.

He knew that once he checked in, he would never leave again. So he went home, opened a hundred year old bottle of single malt whiskey, poured himself and his wife a large drink in their crystal glasses, sat on their front porch swing and watched some of the most magnificent sunsets he had ever seen.

Maybe it was because he knew his time was almost up, or perhaps it was the alcohol, but he had never seen the horizon so intense with scarlet hues. For the briefest of moments, everything was right and he knew what heaven must be like.

He stayed at home as long as he could, but when he felt himself fading away, he gave Brooke his family coat of arms ring that never came off his finger and she put it beside an old, gold watch in her jewellery box. He took one last look around the house, felt the cool breeze caress his wrinkled face and then checked himself back into the hospital's palliative care wing.

It felt strange, but he was happy not to be alone anymore.

For as long as he could remember, he had always been alone. As a child he had spent countless hours by himself in his room, reading about the adventures of others. All of his friends were there every time he cracked the spine of a book, and welcomed him like a lost brother. They never laughed at his crossed teeth or made fun of how scrawny he was, and they didn't always pick him last for their team during gym class.

Books allowed him to forget about the harshness of the world for a while and enter a place where it was as normal to see a dragon fly by as it was to see a shimmering sunset. They made him feel part of something, a sensation all too rare when he was not in his room.

The one exemption to his law of loneliness was his pet dog, Muffin. The Muffster, as he liked to call him, was a medium sized black poodle with a white chin. He could still remember the day he first met his best friend. He was five and his parents had bundled both him and his brother in the back seat of the family car and had driven to a nearby city with a large Ferris wheel. The sky was grey and he had stared at the moving circular silhouette while his dad disappeared for a few minutes. Suddenly the back door opened and a furry bundle of excitement jumped into the back seat with his brother and him. He remembered shouting, "Wow! A dog!" and was met with a quick lick on his cheek.

The years passed by slowly, something he had never figured out. As a child, a day could seem as long as a year, but as he grew older, the exact opposite seemed to happen and Muffin was always by his side.

The poodle had gotten fat over the years, especially after being de-nutted, but if you think about it, it makes perfect sense. If he were to have his balls eliminated from the game, he would gain weight too! After all, there really isn't much left to do otherwise.

Muffin was always there to meet him at the door with a wagging tail, and even as he grew older and it became more difficult for him to walk up the stairs, he still did it. The Muffinator had lost his front teeth and he would laugh as his tongue would flick out of his mouth and around his beard, just like a snake.

Then early in October, fourteen years after he had first met his best friend and only three days after his nineteenth birthday, he had to say goodbye. Muffin had grown sick over the years and cancer had spread to his lungs. He was coughing all the time and had to be carried up the stairs at night because of the arthritis in his legs. He had thrown up on the upstairs carpet that morning and it was obvious he was in pain, so his parents had decided it was time to put Muffin to sleep.

It was the hardest thing he had ever experienced to that point in his life and he didn't know how to handle it. He had gone out to his car to compose himself and try to get a grip on his emotions when the house door opened and Muffin came bounding outside, tailing wagging and excited to go for a car ride. He opened the back door to his parents car and Muffin jumped in without a second thought, dragging his leash behind him. He remembered leaning into the car and wrapping his arms around Muffin's soft fur and giving him a giant hug one last time. He felt so small in his arms and he remembered whispering something that was meant only for them and no one else. The tears came on unexpectedly and powerfully that he could not control himself. He reached out and gave Muffin's head a scratch behind the ears, just the way he liked it and closed the door.

Later that day he woke up from a nap and heard the sound of Muffin's dog tags coming down the hallway. For the briefest of moments he thought that he had dreamed everything and the Muffster was coming for a belly rub. Instead it was his mom carrying Muffin's collar. She gave him one of the tags and his brother, who took Muffin's death the hardest, got his collar and tag.

That was the first time anyone he had ever cared about had left him, and he wanted to make sure it was the last time. He swore that he would never let anyone get that close again. He would control everything, that way he could not be hurt by someone's leaving. It was then that he decided to go into business.

He hadn't always been successful in the business world, not by a long shot. He had failed more times than he could count, but he would always try again and again until he succeeded.

The bitterness of his first venture still remained fresh on the back of his tongue, even though it happened decades before when he was in his mid twenties. He had tried to open a series of doughnut stores in the United Kingdom because they simply did not exist.

He spent over a year scouting out retail locations, consulting the local municipalities about zoning restrictions, contacting suppliers, designing his own flavour of coffee and tea at a local importer, polling the public on their desire for such a business and crunching series of numbers to discover if the venture was even economically feasible.

He would spend all his spare time working dead end jobs for minimum wage while his mates laughed at his choice of careers. In the space of twelve months he worked as a secretary for a slumlord housing corporation, manager of an exclusively gay bar and as a telephone psychic, even though he had no psychic ability whatsoever.

He had the biggest problem with the telephone psychic job because he felt as though he were exploiting lonely people's need to talk to someone. These unsuspecting fools were paying ten dollars per minute to hear "readings" from people who were working in a small room beneath a pet store. He was supposed to keep them on the line for a minimum of twenty minutes each by reading from a prepared script and then suggesting after that perhaps the "crystals" might shed even more light on their situation, which was also read from a prepared script!

He questioned the morality of what they were doing to his manager and was told they were simply filling a need for people who had questions in their lives. He kept his mouth shut, but quit shortly thereafter upon watching a co-worker keep an old lady on the phone for over an hour talking about her lack of finances!

Luckily it was shortly after this point that his number crunching was completed and he discovered, much to his pleasure, that even at a fifty percent sell ratio of his lowest, conservative estimate, he would still make a profit. His biggest profit maker was the coffee because each pot would cost only twenty-five cents to brew and could be sold for five dollars, including cups and condiments.

Yes, he could truly taste the money waiting for him, and it tasted sweet. He had plans in place to expand across the entire United Kingdom within ten years of opening his first store.

With all of his hard data in tow, he made an appointment with the local business development bureau and presented his plans to a group of people in the early summer. It was an excellent presentation and he thought he answered all their questions well and backed everything up with his year of research; which is why their answer caught him so off guard.

They refused to loan him the necessary start up capital because they did not believe that people would drive two minutes out of their way to get a cup of coffee and a doughnut. He tried to explain that if he built it, they would come, but they did not listen. He had been shattered, his dream was in pieces.

He flew back to North America the next week and went back to University to complete his degree.

Years later he had returned to the city that had spurned him and discovered, much to his bitterness, that in the precise spot he had researched, stood a busy doughnut store complete with drive through.

He wasn't happy.

No, he wasn't happy at all.

Obviously, somebody took his research and used it. He had no proof of who it was, but he had a pretty good idea. Legal actions would solve nothing because it would come down to his word against a respected member of the business community. In otherwords, he was screwed.

It took him years to discover what had happened and who the rat was that took his idea, but in the end he did find out. By that point in time he had become very successful and able to excerpt considerable influence on his own. He found out who it was, bought controlling stock in the company, purchased the man's mortgage from the bank and then fired him and called in his loans on the same day.

He made sure the man knew who was responsible for situation and drew great pleasure from the look of recognition in the man's eyes when he clued in who it was.

He always tried to handle himself fairly and equitably, both in business and in life, but there were always those people who seemed to equate his fairness with weakness and tried to knock out the blocks from under him. In times like that he was forced to become a prick and destroy people and companies to such an extent that the rest of the business world would think twice before crossing him.

He was developing the reputation of a shark in the business world because of how he would show no mercy toward a wounded opponent. If only they knew that his resilience was brought about more from surviving many near death experiences than his betrayal with the doughnut store.

How he survived this long was anyone's guess. By all rights he should have been killed on at least three separate occasions dating back to his teenage years.

The first time he had managed to thwart Death's plans for himself was when he was seventeen years old. He had been driving too fast down the most dangerous highway in North America when it happened. He was in the passing lane, behind a big, white cube van that refused to move out of the way, when he made the near fatal error of looking over his right shoulder to see if there was room for him to cut in. Precisely at that point in time, the cube van decided to jam on its brakes.

Everything moved in slow motion.

He immediately cut the wheel to the right and darted across two lanes of traffic and hit the dirt shoulder of the road, where he whipped the wheel back to the left, which kicked out the back end of the car and sent it shooting back across the lanes of traffic and directly toward the concrete divider. He spun the wheel back, missed the guard-rail by a few inches and yanked up the emergency brake. The car's wheels locked up and he did several complete spins on the dry asphalt before coming to a complete stop, straddling both lanes and looking out his driver's door window at two transport trucks bearing down on him.

He remembered thinking that he was dead. No fear or sadness, just that thought.

Somehow, and he didn't know quite how, he managed to get off to the side of the road without being hit. He immediately reached into the back seat with shaking hands and pulled out the bible he kept there. He still wasn't sure if it had anything to do with his survival, but just in case it did, he always travelled with one ever since.

Years later he had been the passenger in the car of his best friend, Beac and they had been heading home, late at night after a business meeting in a nearby city. They had decided to take a back, country road to save some time so they could make the last feature at the local strip club.

Now anyone who has ever driven through the countryside at night knows that there are no street lights or any other form of illumination besides the moon. As luck, or lack thereof, would have it, this was a moonless night and the light from the stars had been obscured by an overcast sky. It was so completely devoid of light, that even sitting in his car, they could barely see their hands in front of their faces.

They were listening to a rock and country mixed tape, zipping along a gravel road between two fields of corn when suddenly he heard the clattering of hooves and a full grown deer jumped in front of the car.

It was just a flash, a mere moment in time, but the picture was still burned in his mind. The glistening darkness of the deer's eye, the sharpness of its antlers, the matted colour of its fur and its immense size, all things that should have been the last thing he saw in this life.

There wasn't time to swerve or even slow down, it happened that quickly. Again, he swore that they were dead, and by all rights they should have been. The car's bumper should have clipped the deer's legs and the entire animal should have come smashing through the windshield, killing them both instantly.

But as quickly as the deer had appeared, it was gone, back into the darkness of the country night. Just like before, he defied all odds and escaped without a single scratch.

Several years later, at the beginning of his business career, he decided to go back to the United Kingdom on vacation. He had always been drawn to the Highlands of Scotland, and in particular the Isle of Skye, and he did not know why. So he had booked a guided tour with a reputable agency located in the heart of Edinburgh and went exploring. He saw where several films were shot, abandoned castles, Loch Ness and even got the chance to put on a red wig with matching kilt.

Finally he made it to the Highlands and they were every bit as magnificent as he had envisioned. Great, rolling hills of green erupted from the craggy landscape like the teeth of some forgotten giant, and everywhere he looked there were hairy cows or "coos" as the locals called them, and herds of sheep.

It was a beautiful day, the sky was a light blue and fluffy, white clouds drifted lazily by on gentle air currents, and the group had the opportunity to go hiking along the cliffs. They had been warned by the tour guide to be careful because many years before, an international student had slipped and fallen to his death along that very path.

He remembered laughing at the image that popped into his head of some person, hanging onto the side of the mountain, surrounded by those creepy, bug eyed, hairy cows just staring at him, innocently chewing their cud.

He couldn't understand what kind of loser would fall off a cliff, especially such a well travelled one. Then when he saw what they were supposed to walk along, it became all too clear.

There were dirt paths, about a foot across, cut into the side of the mountain without a guide rail or safety rope. The path climbed slowly to several hundred feet in the air and there was an almost ninety-degree drop off only a few inches to the right.

About forty-five minutes into the hike, he was admiring the view and thinking about how easy it would be for somebody to go over the edge when he stumbled and brought his full weight down on the outside of his left ankle. He heard a "pop" and before he knew what was going on, the edge of the path came rushing up to meet him and he felt himself going over the edge.

Far below him were patches of jagged rocks, jutting from the loamy soil like the tips of spears and again, he thought he was dead. It was at this time that he swore he heard a voice tell him to spread out his bodyweight like he was on ice and latch on.

It was definitely weird, but he immediately did it and managed to catch himself on the lip of the cliff before he went all the way over. The Aussies he was with helped him stand up and get back down the mountainside. He would have done it under his own power, but he had torn all the ligaments on his left ankle except the Achilles tendon and every time he raised his leg, his foot would snap up several seconds later. The pain was so intense that he actually ran out of vulgarities to curse after only a few minutes.

Thump-thump. Thump-thump. Thump-thump.

"What were you just thinking about?" asked Brooke.

At the sound of her voice, he jumped and realised he had been day dreaming. He smiled and said, "I was just trying to figure out how I've managed to survive this long."

Brooke nodded her head in agreement and replied, "I don't know, but with all the stories you've told me, your guardian angel must have been working overtime!"

I WAS.

"Yeah, he should probably ask for a raise. And do you know what the strange thing is?"

"What?"

"In spite of surviving all those attempts on my life, you are the one that truly saved me in the end."

Brooke's eyes began to glisten as he continued, "I don't know what my life would have been like if I hadn't met you. Probably full of hot, young, big breasted women that just wanted to use me for my money. Yep, it would have been a great life."

Brooke looked momentarily shocked, but when she saw his eyes glinting mischievously, she replied, "Just for that, I will make sure that we end up together in the next life as well."

He smiled and whispered, "I wouldn't have it any other way. I can still remember how we met."

He closed his eyes and let the memories of the day that would change his life forever wash over him.

Their first meeting was quite unexpected, as most things of this nature were. He was scouting some property near the city centre that was full of abandoned and burned out warehouses, when a bum approached him and asked for some spare change.

The man was covered in dirt and smelled like a dung heap. What hair he had was white and greasy, his clothing was old, threadbare and stuffed with newspapers to help keep him warm. Deep wrinkles carved his face and the eyes that stared out from beneath them were milky and sad.

This creature disgusted him and it was all he could do to stop from vomiting. He felt himself cringe inwardly as he looked at that loss of humanity and he knew that the expression on his face mirrored what he was thinking.

His initial reaction would be to ignore the person and walk away, or to belittle them about not having a job and sponging off the honest tax-payers like himself. He felt his mouth open to begin the tirade, but as he glanced at the charred structure before him, a strange chill ran down his spine and he stopped.

Instead he heard himself ask the bum what he needed the money for, and the man replied it was for something to drink to help keep him warm at night. He asked the man why he did not just sleep in the nearby shelter and he was informed that he did not have the money to pay for a cot.

At this point in time, he would normally give the bum a few dollars and dismiss them like a teacher would a child, but something told him to help this man out. He extended his hand and introduced himself.

"I'm Lee."

The old man looked in disbelief at the outstretched hand for a moment and then grasped it with his own, "My name is Paul."

"It is a pleasure to meet you, Paul. I won't help you buy alcohol, but if you would be interested in a cup of coffee and a bite to eat, there is a coffee house just up the road."

Paul stared at him, trying to figure out his intentions, but finally he agreed and they crossed the road for a coffee. As soon as they entered the coffee house, everyone inside became really quiet and he could see all of them staring at Paul. For the first time in years, he felt embarrassed; not for himself, but for this man beside him. To Paul's credit, he threw back his shoulders, stood straight and ignored the looks of disgust from the crowd.

They were about to order when the owner of the store approached, pulled him to the side and said, "Excuse me, but I have had several complaints from my regular customers about this," he paused, "this "person" and to be honest, I do not want him in my establishment. You may stay if you wish, but that waste certainly cannot."

He saw Paul's shoulders hunch forward and felt that familiar sensation of anger bubble to the surface. He turned to the owner and replied, "Let me get this straight. You are throwing this man, who wants nothing more than something hot to eat, out of your establishment because he makes other people uncomfortable? Did I hear you correctly?"

The owner stiffened slightly and replied indignantly, "You most certainly did. You may stay, but I reserve the right to refuse admittance to scum."

He couldn't believe his ears and he felt his face growing red.

"This so called scum is my guest and when you insult the people I am with, you insult me. I don't know who you think you are talking to, but I suggest that you apologise to this man immediately."

The owner's eyes narrowed and he sneered, "I will do no such thing. And for the record, I know who I am talking to; a cocky young man who has not learned his place in the world. Now get out before I call the police and have them escort you out."

He was about to tell the owner exactly what he could do with his supposed place when he felt a surprisingly strong grip on his shoulder. He turned and looked at Paul who was shaking his head.

"It's not worth it," said Paul giving his shoulder a squeeze, "Thanks for trying. Now let's get out of here."

The owner gave them a smug smile as they left and he felt himself shaking with rage at how poorly they had been treated. Then it hit him, this must be exactly how people like Paul felt all the time.

He was ashamed, and decided to do something about it.

"Excuse me for a second Paul," he said, pulling out his cell phone, "I have to make a quick call."

He pressed the number for his office and said, "Brad? It's Lee. You know those properties I'm looking at? Yeah, those ones. I need you to find out who owns the coffee shop just down the road from there and then find out who holds his mortgage. Yes, everything. Then arrange a meeting tomorrow morning with his bank. I want all this guy's property; business, house, car, everything."

"Wait Lee," said Paul, coming to stand beside him.

"Hold on a second Brad."

He turned his attention toward Paul who said, "I know what you are planning on doing. I appreciate the effort, but it's just not worth it."

He paused and then spoke into the phone, "I'll have to call you back."

The old man shook his head and smiled at him. It was one of only a few teeth, but the most genuine one he had seen in quite some time.

"What do you mean it is not worth it?" he asked. "That guy treated you and I like scum. He completely insulted, then dismissed us! I want him to learn that he can't treat people like that."

Paul's smile broadened and he said gently, "Everyone has made mistakes in this life; it is what we do. If I harbour no resentment toward him, you should not. After all, haven't you ever done anything bad in your life?"

A chill ran down his spine and he was flooded with images of his past. Some he welcomed, while others had been buried so far down that he barely recognised them. He slowly nodded his head and said, "You're right. But I still want to make sure he comes to realise the error of his ways, and I cannot think of a better way than buying out all his outstanding loans and foreclosing on him tomorrow. I want to have him suffer like the weasel that he is."

Paul's face grew sad. He shook his head and said quietly, "It's not up to you to balance out the universe; everything has a habit of taking care of itself. I'm worried about you, Lee."

"Why? You don't even know me."

"But, you see, I do. I was you many years ago. A mansion, sports cars, servants, I had it all, or at least I thought I did. I had the choice about what mark I would leave on the world, and I chose poorly. I lost everything in the blink of an eye, but in doing so I gained the world. What mark do you want to leave on the world after you are gone?"

He always thought that the secret of his legacy would be money and power, but after seeing somebody standing before him that could very well represent his future, he was no longer certain, so he said, "I'm not sure."

Paul nodded his head in agreement and said, "That I believe. In time you will know, but remember to always pay attention to the situations around you because you never know what part you might play."

Another shiver raced down his spine and he said, "Thanks for the advice. I'd like to return the gesture in kind. The cup of coffee seems to have failed miserably, so what do you say about going to the shelter and allowing me to get you a place to keep warm?"

Paul sighed contentedly and said, "It's a deal."

They walked together down the dirty sidewalk and talked as though they had known each other for years. Soon they reached the nearby shelter and he paused to take it all in.

A broken neon sign did its best to flash its welcome to the countless homeless people spread beneath the man-made glow. The building was old and worn, but someone had done their best to lovingly repair the doorway and patch the holes in the concrete. The entrance was spotlessly clean and warm, yellow light spilled out from behind the frosted panes of glass.

He bounded up the steps and held the door open for Paul, who paused at the entrance before shuffling inside. He followed and stopped in his tracks.

The room was plain and the carpet threadbare, but what took his breath away was the figure behind the antique wooden counter. Her back was turned to them and she was lost in thought, absent mindedly stroking what appeared to be a man's gold pocket watch.

"Hello Brooke," said Paul.

At the sound of his voice, Brooke jumped and turned around, placing the watch in her pants pocket in one fluent motion.

Their eyes locked.

She was gorgeous. Big, blue eyes stared at him while long locks of blond hair fell in waves past her shoulders. For the first time in his life, he did not know what to say. He just stared with a strange smile on his face.

Time seemed to slow as she held out her hand and said, "Hi. My name's Brooke. What is yours?"

"I'm Lee," he replied as he reached out his own hand, never taking his eyes off her. When their hands met, he felt a surge of electricity and from the corner of his eye, he saw Paul smile.

Thump-thump. Thump-thump. Thump-thump.

He looked up and stared at the woman who had stood by his side for all those years and smiled. Time had change her blond hair to white, and wrinkles had replaced the smooth skin of youth, but he still saw the same woman he fell in love with at the homeless shelter all those decades ago.

It had taken several years for him to realise the error of his ways. The secret of his legacy was not money and power. The true secret of life was family. Their children, grandchildren and even great grandchildren were what made them truly wealthy.

After he met her, he always tried to live each day to the fullest. He made sure to tell her how much he loved her every chance he had because you never know what moment would be your last.

Dying wasn't the hard part; he was pretty sure he'd be good at it. The biggest difficulty was leaving those he cared about behind as he discovered the answer to the ultimate mystery by himself. Every person dies alone; it is in how we greet our end that defines the true measure of our lives.

He had a very full life and in spite of all the challenges he experienced, if he were presented with the opportunity to do it all again, he would not change a thing because it brought him to her.

His only regret about dying was the knowledge that he would not be able to hold her in his arms again; at least not for a while.

They had always snuggled, and as disturbing as their children found it, he would always grab her bum every chance he got. He couldn't help himself, he was a butt man and quite proud of it. Plus, he liked how squeamish it made their children every time he went in for a quick feel.

He opened his eyes and smiled at Brooke.

"That is an evil smile if ever I saw one. What are you up to?" asked Brooke suspiciously.

"Without my Viagra, not much. Not much at all!" he responded.

Brooke gasped in mock shock and playfully chided him, "Behave yourself! We are in the middle of a hospital!"

"I'm just saying, it would probably be like trying to shoot pool with a rope, but if you fancy a quickie, I'm sure I can rise to the occasion."

"I'm sure you can."

Even now at the end, after so many years, he still found her desirable. True, their bodies had been falling apart for a long time, but that was what kept things interesting. They had always told their children that the secret of keeping things hot between the sheets was comfort, both with yourself and your partner.

He chuckled when he remembered their reactions. One looked deeply disturbed and the other said he lost fifty IQ points after hearing that.

Yep, they truly were his kids. He never wanted offspring, but now he could not imagine his life without them in it.

Neither John nor Ian was there at the moment. He had sent them home to be with their families because he did not want their last memories of him to be like this; hooked up to machines with tubes hanging out of nearly every orifice of his body.

Both sons hated the hospital as much, if not more, than he did and every moment they spent inside was something he refused to put them through. They would stay by his bedside until the very end and not say a word about their discomfort, but it was not necessary. Perhaps it was selfish on his part, but they had already said their good-byes a few days before.

He had taken everyone out for dinner and had given each of them, their wives and his grandchildren a huge hug. There were a few tears, but as he looked at his family sitting around that table in the restaurant, he felt a surge of pride about how everything turned out in his life. It had been a good life.

YES IT HAD.

"Did you say something?" he asked, focusing his eyes on Brooke.

"No," she replied, "I was just watching you."

"I thought I heard a voice," he said, gently sinking back into the comfortable bed. "This dying thing is really playing tricks with my mind."

Brooke flinched when he said the word dying and she turned her face to try and hide the tears that were streaming from her eyes.

With great difficulty he raised his shaking hand and laid it on her, gently interlacing his fingers with hers. At his touch, she stopped picking her nails, turned back to him and smiled with her eyes glistening.

"Hey pretty lady."

"Hey."

"Don't worry," he said giving her fingers a squeeze, "It's not that bad, really. It feels kind of familiar. Does that sound strange?"

Brooke shook her head softly and replied, "Not at all, it is just who you are and I wouldn't have it any other way."

He was growing sleepy and it was becoming more and more difficult to keep his eyes open.

This was it, he could tell.

He felt himself drifting away, sinking into his bed. Everything sounded distant, as if he were listening through cotton. It wasn't getting dark as he had always assumed, rather the surrounding light seemed to be growing brighter. But it wasn't a harsh brightness, it was warm and welcoming. Strange. In the distance he could hear the heart monitor, relentlessly monitoring every second left of his life.

Thump-thump. Thump-thump. Thump-thump.

He always thought he would be nervous or scared, but he wasn't. That's the part that confused him. If anything, he was happy and excited, just like after summer camp when he was coming home. Maybe that was it - he was going home.

YOU ARE.

He could feel his breathing slowing. It wouldn't be long now.

Thump-thump........thump-thump......

He could feel another presence close by, in the same room and just out of sight. It was familiar and welcoming.

His lips were dry and his tongue did not want to respond. He forced his eyes to focus on his wife and she smiled.

"I love you," he whispered quietly.

She leaned forward and kissed him on the forehead. Her lips felt warm and soft, just like the first time he had discovered them many years before. She moved close to his ear and spoke so only he could hear, "I love you too. You can leave now, it's alright. You make sure to come get me when it is my turn. I'll see you again."

Thump......thump.......thump......

Here we go.

Thump.........

Why did he smell quiche?

ACT SEVEN

The wail of the flat line siren faded away, as did the heaviness of his body. He blinked one last time and suddenly found himself standing at the foot of the bed, watching the used husk of his body go through the motions of winding down its life.

It was really strange to watch himself die, and yet strangely reminiscent of taking your favourite vehicle to the junkyard when its time was up. What used to be his body smiled gently and then did not move again.

He was dead.

It wasn't quite what he expected. Somehow he had hoped that there would be someone there to take him to heaven because he didn't know the way. Instead, he was in a palliative care hospital room, aware of everything that was going on around him, yet separate and alone.

"You will never be alone Lee," said a deep voice from behind him.

Lee turned toward the voice and immediately recognised the presence that he had felt in the room a few minutes earlier. An old man with a long beard and unkempt hair stood at the doorway of the room, smiling warmly at him.

He knew that man.

"Yes, you met me a long time ago on a dirty street in a horrid part of town. You showed me kindness and I introduced you to your wife," said the figure, slowly shuffling into the room.

"Of course," said Lee quickly extending his hand, "Paul! I always wondered what happened to you. You disappeared right after introducing Brooke and I in that run down homeless shelter she was running. I'm glad I finally get the chance to repay you for the fifty years of marriage we endured together."

Paul stopped in his tracks and momentarily looked concerned as Lee drew back his fist and shot the other arm forward, wrapped it around Paul's shoulders and drew him in for a huge hug.

"Thank you for letting me love such a wonderful woman," Lee whispered into Paul's ear, "She was the best part of me, you know?"

Paul gently patted Lee on the back and said, "I know, that's why we didn't take you home immediately. Tim thought you deserved another few moments with her, and after the amazing prank he played on me, I thought it best to stay on his good side."

"Tim?" asked Lee, squinting his eyes in thought, "Why do I know that name? Is he an angel?"

"I guess it depends on who you ask," replied Paul, disengaging himself from Lee's grip and taking a step back toward the doorway which had started to glow.

Lee felt himself drawn toward the light, but he also felt compelled to stay beside the woman who had shared everything with him. She knew all about his past; every dirty, underhanded and morally questionable thing he had ever done in his lifetime, and still she loved him for who he was. She was his everything and he was worried about how she would manage without him.

He knew the boys would keep an eye on her, of that he had no doubt, but it was her strong willed nature that concerned him most. There were times when he often thought that it would be easier to give a piranha a root canal than try and change her mind once it was made up. Hopefully Ian or John would come up with a way to keep her interested in staying healthy, like a pet of some kind. But that was out of his hands now, he would have to have faith in the way their kids had been raised.

"Lee, it's time to go," said Paul gently from the doorway.

The light had grown so much brighter that he could no longer see Paul, instead just a silhouette remained. Lee stuck out his bottom lip and nodded his head in agreement. It was time to go home and he had said his goodbyes, but somehow it did not make him feel any better about leaving.

He walked over to the side of the bed where Brooke sat, holding the hand of his empty body and sobbing uncontrollably. He reached out his hand and tried to wipe the tears from her wrinkled face, but he could not touch her. Instead he leaned down and gently placed a kiss on her cheek.

As he turned to walk away, he saw her smile and touch her cheek. Brooke closed her eyes and said, "Thank you, Lee. I'll see you again."

Lee found himself choking up and he tried to smile, but his eyes burned and his bottom lips quivered. He would see her again.

He promised.

Lee walked toward where Paul was waiting, and with one last look behind, stepped into the brightly glowing, soft light.

Its radiance washed over him like a warm summer rain and it enveloped his ethereal form, Lee felt as though he were a part of it, a part of a universal story. Everywhere around him he felt the welcoming presence of people he had known, family and acquaintances long gone. He swore he could even hear the rattle of Muffin's collar and his soft fur against his fingertips.

He felt a joy unmatched by anything except the first time he had seen his children. It was almost overwhelming, but he knew that he was welcome.

He knew he was home.

"Your work is done," said a voice from the light, "It's time to rest. You never have to work again."

He knew that voice. But from where?

Suddenly a bright lemon shirt appeared being worn by a man with fluffy white wings. He appeared young and lean and had slicked back dark hair and perfectly trimmed handle bar moustache. His crisp black dress pants made a swishing sound as he approached and the gleam from his highly polished, black leather dress shoes created a halo effect around his entire torso.

Lee was sure that he knew him and in the blink of an eye, everything came rushing back to him. He remembered it all; every lifetime, every sensation, every experience that life had to offer. Some memories were hard to deal with, while others, like Brooke, required no effort and were the sweetest of all.

He had lived and died many times before, but no experience had been quite like this one. The cafe was no where to be found, nor was there any sign of the tables, the overstuffed chairs of any of Tim's wonderful quiche. Where was he?

"That's easy," said Tim, as he stopped in front of him and smiled warmly, "You are back at the same place where you started, just on the other side of everything you ever knew."

Bal looked at Tim, shook his head and said, "What? Try explaining this to me in English. I can think as deeply as the next person, but I would need a lot of beer to understand what you just said."

Tim laughed and replied, "You're so silly, Balthy! Well let me explain quickly before your ride arrives.'

"Ride? Am I going somewhere?"

"Of course. Why wouldn't you be?"

"Huh? I'm getting a headache."

"Don't worry about it, one of Michael's cocktails will fix you up and you will be right as rain in no time. But I digress! Sorry about me being so chatty; I get it from my mother. Anyway, I'm so excited because I just got the word and this has never happened before to someone who had only completed six roles."

"What's happened?" asked Balthazar as he tilted his head to the side.

"Well," said Tim, taking a deep breath and clasping his hands excitedly in front of him, "It's like this. Both the head casting director and Mr. Josephsson were so impressed by the dedication you showed in your last three assignments, that they have decided to promote you to Elite Status!"

"Is that good?"

Tim's eyes bulged out of his head and he gasped, "Good? That is unheard of! What that means is that you have the ability to pick and choose whatever role you want from this point on! Do you understand what I am saying? You can now influence the course of the story itself! You can go anywhere, do everything or do nothing, the choice is yours!"

"I could do anything?"

Tim nodded and whispered, "Anything. Maybe you could be a pirate, surrounded by big, burly, sweaty men for months at a time. Remember, the stories are always being rewritten, so you have the chance to try different things and still be within the confines of the story itself. This story has been rewritten twice already! The choice is yours."

A surge of excitement shot down his spine as the truth of the words Tim uttered sank in. He could do anything he wanted. No longer would he have to have to be a whore, professor, loser, writer, bum or...or....a businessman.

I'll see you again.

What an amazing opportunity. He could finally have everything he wanted.

I promise.

"But what about Brooke, uh, I mean Cera? Will she be able to come with me?"

The smile faded from Tim's face and he said, "No. The offer was for you and you alone. Cera is not quite ready to go where you will be. She has several more roles to complete before she would even be considered for such a responsibility."

This was the ultimate chance, something everyone hoped to attain someday, and now it was within his grasp, all he had to do was reach out and take it. Cera had caused him nothing but problems for several lifetimes and beyond, so he didn't even know why he was having a problem deciding. He knew that she would take the position without a second though and leave him with his berries dangling in the breeze.

But then again, she did turn down several key roles for an opportunity to work with him again, and she did save him as much as he saved her that night in the burning building. He had returned to Earth to work with her and through some divine intervention on the part of Paul, he met her again and they had spent over fifty years together. She had borne him two wonderful sons and believed in him no matter what. They had not been apart for longer than a few days during that entire period of time and he no longer recognised where he stopped and she began.

I promise.

Bal shook his head and tried to remind himself that it was just a story and they were just actors in someone else's play. It didn't matter what happened on Earth. All that was important was a lie.

But he knew it wasn't.

"Can I ask you a question, Tim?" asked Balthazar, locking eyes with the angel who had such an impact on his life experiences.

"Of course Balthy, what's on your mind?" replied Tim, absent mindedly stroking the sides of the moustache.

"This is a really rare offer, right?"

"Extremely rare!"

"Then it would be bad for me to turn it down, huh?"

The colour drained from Tim's face and he stopped touching his face. He became as solid as a statue and stared in disbelief at Bal.

"No, it's bad to turn down a twenty percent off clothing sale, this would be catastrophic! There would be a very good chance that you would never work again! You could be written out of the story, or even made to start back at the beginning. Think about it, Balthy."

Tim was right. He knew that to turn down such an important assignment would be foolhardy at best and stupid to say the least.

It was everything he wanted.

She was everything he wanted.

It was everything he needed.

She was everything he needed.

It represented his future.

She represented his future.

"What should I do, Tim?"

Tim blinked, took a step back and smiled at Bal.

"I'm sorry Balthy, but I cannot help you. The writer of our story is watching, the pen paused above the parchment, waiting to write what you and you alone must decide."

Suddenly the same bus he arrived on appeared alongside him, and with a *whoosh* opened its doors. The smell of cinnamon wafted from the bus's interior and suddenly he was staring into the fiery green eyes of Elley.

"Perhaps I can make you a better offer, Balthazar," said Elley seductively as she glided down the stairs of the bus and came to rest beside Bal. Her dagger like fingernails gently traced a pattern on his shoulder as she hissed, "I have been instructed by Mr. Cypher to give you anything you want."

Balthazar tilted his head toward her and said, "Anything?"

"Yes, anything your heart desires. The choicest of roles that will guarantee you money, power, even love."

"Cera?"

Elley nodded and smiled.

"But what do you want in exchange?"

Elley's smile widened.

"Nothing much at all. In exchange for being our new star and having whatever role you desire, we request that you sign an exclusive, binding contract for the term of your career; that's it."

Balthazar stuck out his bottom lip and his brow furled in thought. What should he do? If he took Tim's offer, he could help to influence the course of the story itself, but Cera would be alone forever. If he took Elley's offer, he could also have whatever story he wanted, and he could keep his promise to Cera, but he would have to sign an exclusive contract. Still, she would be with him.

Tim looked at Bal and Elley, then took a step forward and said, "What are you doing, Balthy? You cannot seriously be considering her offer! I know you love her, but this is not the way. You have to have faith in the story."

Sensing she was winning, Elley pressed her advantage. She smirked at Tim and said, "Did he tell you what the story has in store for your love, your Cera?"

"What is she talking about, Tim?"

Before he could answer, Elley continued, "Years have passed on Earth in the brief time we have been talking. She is much older now, much more vulnerable. In fact, it has been scripted that she is going to die in a home invasion, alone and scared. The men will rape her repeatedly and then take their time killing her. It will be awful."

Balthazar's eyes opened wide in shock and he stared at Tim, "Is that true?"

"Don't listen to her, Balthy," said Tim as he gave Elley a dirty look. "You must have faith that everything will turn out the way it is meant to be."

"Sure, faith," sneered Elley. "What has faith ever gotten you? All of your roles have ended badly for you alone! You've been abused, used and discarded by everyone you have met, and all you have to show for six lifetimes is a broken heart and drained spirit! Don't you find it interesting that the only happiness you experienced was when you worked for us?"

Tim moved forward and said, "She's lying, Balthy, twisting the truth."

Elley gasped, "I wouldn't do that! I have far too much respect for him. He has a great future ahead of him with us, and there is nothing you can do about it."

"Back off, hag," warned Tim, his movements becoming more rigid and less flamboyant. The very air around him became electric and Balthazar saw, for the first time, hardness in Tim's eyes. Even Elley sensed that she might have pressed things too far, but she was too close to stop now.

"How can it be scripted that the woman you love is going to be raped and murdered in the very home that you built with love? How is that right?"

Tim's face took on the hardness of marble and he seemed to grow in height as he said, "Only the writer knows what happens, Balthy. Remember the story is always being rewritten. You must believe that everything turns out as it should."

Elley glanced past Tim, into the emptiness and cautions, "You are almost out of time! There they are and there she is, sitting in her favourite chair with a cup of tea! She does not have a chance!"

"Balthy...."

Elley moved quickly, like an excited squirrel and hissed into Balthazar's ear, "If you choose us, you can stop it! You can save her, just as she saved you!"

Tim looked with concern from Balthazar to Elley and back again.

"You don't know what you are agreeing to Balthy!"

"Don't listen to him. You can stop it. You can change the story!"

"No, Balthy! Don't do it! You will be written out of the story!"

"Don't worry, we will write you back in!"

"You will never work again!"

"Yes you will. You time is almost up!"

"Do you want to give up forever?" yelled Tim.

Forever.

For love.

"Yes!" hissed Elley, "Do it! Don't you love her? Stop them!"

"No! Balthy! Please! Believe in the story!"

She was his missing piece.

She made him complete.

They had spent so many lifetimes together, how could he leave her now?

He promised.

I'll see you again.

"Ten seconds."

Balthazar turned toward Elley and said, "How can I save her?"

"Choose to fall. Close your eyes and feel yourself there and you will be."

"She is lying to you! Choose the bus. Have faith!"

"Choose to stop them! Choose love!" snarled Elley, stepping between Tim and Balthazar. "Time's up! Make your choice!"

He could feel a welcoming presence from within the bus. He was drawn to it and knew that as soon as he boarded, everything would be complete.

She made him complete.

He couldn't leave her alone.

Balthazar stared at the open doors of the bus for what seemed like an eternity. He had to choose.

He took a deep breath, closed his eyes and moved forward.

The doors closed and the bus drove off.

Tim smiled, nodded his head and disappeared.

The writer's pen touched the parchment.

THE FRIEND

The last five years had been difficult for her, especially this day. It was his birthday, and even though he was gone, she continued to celebrate the life of the person that changed her life forever.

The room was wrapped in the lengthening shadows of the evening and the light from a single candle on top of a tiny chocolate cake danced along the inside cover of the gold watch placed beside it.

She gently traced the faded picture of an unknown lady with her finger and sighed. She knew nothing about the lady except she was well loved, much the same way as she had been.

"Well, Happy Birthday Lee," said Brooke as she leaned forward to blow out the candle. She felt a cold nose press against her hand, followed by an abnormally large, flat head in search of a scratch.

"What do you want, Rosco? I wasn't talking to you."

Rosco's head tilted to the side and the way his jowels hung down, she could swear that he was smiling at her.

"I just fed you an hour ago. You can't be hungry again."

His head tilted to the other side and he sat down in front of her, dark brown eyes flicking from her to the cake on the table. He placed one massive paw gently on her thigh and licked his chops.

"I don't think so! You know that chocolate is bad for dogs. You can't suck me into giving you a piece."

Rosco's stumpy tail whipped excitedly back and forth on the wooden floor and he tugged on her leg with his paw. His brow moved up and down in what she was certain was an attempt to look so cute that she would give in to his sweettooth.

"Just because you got me three years in a row does not mean that I am a push over this year!"

Twenty minutes later Rosco was laying at her feet in the family room, licking his chops and burping contentedly.

Brooke placed her dessert plate on the coffee table beside her and settled back into her chair with a nice cup of hot tea. She looked down at the animal that had outsmarted her again and smiled. Whomever said that boxers were as smart as a rock never met this one. She had spent months trying to train him before she realized that, in fact, he had been training her.

Rosco was truly a suck, a one hundred thirty pound drool machine that liked to cuddle and thought that he was a lap dog. It was her own fault.

When he was a puppy, she would sit with his tiny head nestled in her neck and rock him back and forth for hours. He loved to cuddle and seemed to forget that he wasn't a tiny puppy anymore. Every chance he got, he would still try and climb up her by putting one paw on each shoulder and hoisting himself up. Her children were worried that he would hurt her, but Rosco was so gentle that it never happened.

He had been a gift from John and Ian at Christmas the year that Lee had died. It had been a difficult period for her, in fact it still was. She had been feeling down because she had been going through his closet, gathering up his clothing to give away to the shelters, when she caught a whiff of his cologne and images from past holidays came streaming back.

Lee had always loved getting presents, especially on his birthday and Christmas. In fact, he would always start the countdown to each of them with three months to go. He would post reminders for everyone about how many shopping days remained until the "big occasion" as he called them.

Every Christmas morning, from their very first together until their very last, he would be up before everyone and checking out the presents under the tree. She would have to watch him like a hawk because given an opportunity, he would do his best to sneak a peek inside the wrapping paper.

When they had first started dating, she was unaware of both his obsession with presents and his inate ability to move silently around the house. He was truly like a snake and he would have figured out what she had bought for him if she had not accidently walked into the living room as he was reaching for his present.

From that point on it was a game; her cleverness against his sneakiness. Many times he had tried to convince her that she did not need to wrap the gifts right away because he would not look for them, as it would spoil the surprise.

She almost fell for it.

Once.

She had been shopping and was in the back room putting things away, when she caught movement out of the corner of her eye. He had slithered up the stairs and was laying on his belly, peeking around the side of the doorway at her.

She shook her head in amazement and then drew his attention away from the presents by bending over and pretending to do something. She knew he was powerless to resist her butt and it had the desired affect shortly thereafter.

From that point on she had always wrapped the gifts immediately after she purchased them. She would use tape that would change colour if it were removed as well as paper that would mark easily should it be tampered with.

Several times she had heard muttered swearing from the other room and smiled because she knew he had discovered her secret wrapping and was unable to figure a way around it.

This went on for over fifty years and each time he thought he had come up with a way to beat her system, she would simply adapt and change things around. It was a game and she liked to win.

She smiled sadly and started taking his clothing out of the closet and placing everything on their bed. The closet was almost empty when she noticed something large and shiny in the back right hand corner, sticking out from under an old sweatshirt.

She pulled it out of its hiding place and gasped. It was a Christmas present from Lee, one he must have bought when he had checked himself out of the hospital. There was a note attached to it in his handwriting that said:

Hello Pretty Lady! I'm sorry that I won't be able to be there when you open this present, but I want you to know that I love you - I always have. I don't know if there is a heaven, but if there is, I would like to imagine that we could meet at a place like this. Thanks for believing in me when I didn't believe in myself. Merry Christmas Brooke.

Love Lee

Tears came to her eyes as she sat down beside the heap of clothes on the bed, and with shaking hands she tore into the shiny paper. It was a painting of people sitting around tables at an outside cafe under a summer sunset. The mood was serene and all the patrons were smiling, especially the one in the multi-coloured shirt by the cafe's enterance. In the exact center of the painting was an empty table with two chairs that seemed to be waiting to welcome them. It was beautiful.

She went downstairs and hung the painting on the wall, right by her chair and spent the next several hours just staring at it, lost in thought.

She still looked at it everyday, especially on days like this one. It brought her comfort to think that he was there, waiting for her to arrive.

Brooke stretched out a foot to rub the back of Rosco, who had fallen asleep and was snoring loudly. At the feeling of her touch, he raised his head briefly to look at her, put it back on the carpet, passed gas and fell back asleep.

"You stink, dog. That's the last piece of chocolate cake you ever get. Hey, are you listening to me?"

She prodded him again with her toe and he passed gas a second time.

"You really are a big, hairy, drooling machine, aren't you? Lee would have loved you. It's too bad you never got the chance to meet him; you could have contests to see who could out-stink the other one."

Brooke laughed to herself. It was strange the things she remembered about him, including the great pleasure he always received from trying to make her sick to her stomach.

When they had first started dating, she had taken him to her annual family reunion deep in the countryside. There had been a lot of alcohol floating around and she had indulged beyond her usual limit by at least six beers before retiring to their tent for the night. She remembered waking up suddenly with the beer opting for a return visit and she could not find the zipper for the door.

Lee woke up, grinned, said not to worry about it and just puke through the mesh on the tent. He then placed one finger over his lips and pretended to puke, complete with all too realistic sound effects.

She did not find that funny.

After she had eliminated the previous week's worth of food at the nearby creek, she weaved her way through the darkness and back to the conspicouously sealed flap of the tent. In one fluid motion she threw back the flap, saw the white, cheshire cat grin of Lee and immediately wished she hadn't. A stench more putrid than rotten eggs marinated in pig dung leapt out of the warm, moist opening and enveloped her senses. It was so vile that she barely had time to turn her head before she threw up again. All the time Lee was in his sleeping bag laughing hysterically.

She did not find that funny either.

What was it about men that made them want to share such things? She had the opportunity to meet his best friend, Beac, and was amazed to watch those two grown men break wind and then waft it toward the other person so it could be graded.

She remembered asking them why it was fine for men to do it and not women. If only she had a camera with her to record the looks of shock and disgust written on their faces in response to her question. Lee informed her that women could not participate because it was gross. When she told them that it was a double-standard, they asked her what her point was.

They would have loved Rosco as much as she did.

"Isn't that right, buddy? Nana loves you."

Sensing an opportunity for a cuddle, Rosco immediately got up, walked over to the chair and started to climb up.

"No, Rosco, get down."

He placed one massive paw on either side of her and stood up on his hind legs, pushing his flat head into her chest for a scratch.

"Did you hear me? You are too big to be a lapdog."

He looked at her with his big brown eyes and licked her face.

"You are such a suck, you know that?" said Brooke, gently scratching behind his ears. Rosco leaned into her and belched.

"That was pleasant. Thanks for sharing that with me."

She looked at the clock on the wall and was surprised at how late it had gotten. Time had slipped away on her and soon one of her boys would be by to take Rosco for his usual evening walk.

Brooke stroked Rosco's soft fur one more time and then patted him three times on the side, their secret signal for him to get down. Rosco immediately obeyed and watched protectively as she tried to get herself out of her chair.

Lately it had become increasingly difficult to move around the home, and she knew it would be only a matter of time before she could not look after herself any longer and would be forced to rely on others for the first time in her life.

She had always been self sufficent. From the time she had been a little girl, living on the streets in her parents car, to taking over and running a homeless shelter in the worst part of the city, she had always been the responsible one, the rock for others to rest upon. But now, it would seem, that time would do the one thing that she had never allowed to happen; become a burden on her family.

She managed to slowly gain her feet and caught a glimpse of a beautiful sunset streaming through her kitchen window. The ends of the days were always spectacular and from her home, the sunsets seemed to go on forever.

Tonight the colours seemed particularly intense as the bright orange, yellow, red and purle hues swirled together to create something truly special.

She took a deep breath and sighed. Lee always loved the sunset and it did not matter where in the world they were exploring, he would always ensure that it was not missed.

Photos from all their adventures around the world lined the walls of the home. The pyramids, stone henge, the highlands, the great wall of China, they had experienced them all during the day, but it was at this time of night that they truly came alive.

Time was truly an interesting companion. She had once climbed mountains, now she could barely climb the stairs to her bedroom.

Oh well. There was nothing she could do about it now; it was just a fact of life.

Brooke shuffled past Rosco's bowls and noticed that he was running low on water, so she went to the fridge, pulled out the filtered water container and was about to fill up his bowl when there was a brief knock at the front door.

Rosco's ears perked up and he sprang toward the door like a deer, barking and snarling like a posessed beast.

She heard the voice of her youngest son, Ian, shout, "Shaddup! Who do you think you're fooling, huh?"

Immediately the barking stopped, which meant that Rosco was leaning against Ian's knees with his tail going a mile a minute. Her suspicions were realized when she heard, "Yes, it is good to see you too, you slobbering, stinking suck. Who says I want to scratch you? Maybe I'm not interested. Well, O.K., just a quick one. There you go. Now let's go find Nana. Where's Nana?"

There was the sound of a jingling collar and Rosco burst into the kitchen followed by her son. Ian was the spitting image of his father, though he had her eyes and nose. He was a big man by any definition of the word and had a barrel-like chest and hands that were similar to slabs of beef. His hair was short, thick and had been totally white since his mid-thirties, another thing he inherited from his father.

"Hi, mom!" said Ian in a booming voice, "What are you doing?"

"Just giving the dog some water," replied Brooke as she placed the container on the counter.

"Filtered? You know he's a dog, right?"

"Of course I know that. It's just that he prefers the taste of filtered water over the stuff from the tap."

Ian stuck out his bottom lip and shook his head. "That's really sad, Mom."

"Uh huh. Come here so I can hit you," said Brooke, playfully swiping at the air in front of her.

Ian gave her an evil smile and said, "Maybe later. But now I've gotta take this filtered water drinking drool machine out for a walk. We'll be back in a bit. Here, give me a hug."

He leaned his massive form down and gave her a good hug. Ian had always been good at giving hugs and enjoyed getting them as often as he could. In fact, he was always touching his wife in some way and usually grabbed her bum every chance he got. Yes, he truly was his father's son.

"Have fun. If I'm not here when you get back, just come upstairs and get me. I'll make you something to eat."

"O.K. Mom, I'll see you soon. Come on big, hairy, drooly. Let's go for a walk," said Ian as he picked up Rosco's leash and opened the back door.

Normally Rosco would bolt out the door, but for some strange reason, he just tilted his head and stared at her.

"What's wrong, Rosco?" asked Brooke, gingerly reaching down and patting his head.

Rosco tilted his head the other way and whined.

"It's O.K. buddy, I will be just fine until you get back. And if you are a good boy, I will give you some more cake."

Ian raised his left eyebrow and said, "You give him cake as well? This dog eats better than I do! Come on Rosco, let's go."

Rosco looked at Brooke and gently licked her fingertips before walking toward Ian. He paused at the doorway, looked once more at her then trotted outside with Ian close behind.

Brooke watched them disappear into the fields and smiled. She made herself another cup of tea and decided to head upstairs for a quick rest before they returned. She changed into her nightie, pulled back the sheets and slipped into pure comfort. The pillows enveloped her heavy head and she knew it would not be long before she was gone.

Brooke felt herself drifting away, almost like what happened everytime she went to sleep, but this time it felt different somehow; deeper, longer. She snuggled into her side of the bed and pulled the comforter up until it rested just under her chin. A few weeks before she had caught a chill and had been unable to shake it until tonight. Now with a hot cup of tea in her, nestled beneath the softest down in her favourite pajamas, on newly washed, crisp sheets, she felt warm and strangely content.

She sighed and felt her eyes growing heavy. She always welcomed this time of night because it allowed her to forget that she was alone. Familiar faces were always waiting for her in her dreams, and she knew that someday Lee would be there as well.

"I always was, you just didn't see me."

Brooke half opened her eyes and looked in the direction the voice came from. Silhouetted in the doorway of her bedroom stood a familiar figure smiling mischeviously at her.

"Lee?"

"Of course, pretty lady. Were you expecting somebody else? Perhaps a naked, muscular angel?" asked Lee, slowly strolling into the room and stopping by the head of the bed.

"That would have been nice, but I guess you will have to do. You came back for me?"

A surge of emotion washed over her and she felt herself begin to cry.

Lee reached down, gently wiped the tears from her wrinkled cheeks, smiled and said, "Of course I did. After all, I promised. Besides, I will let you in on a little secret."

"What's that?" asked Brooke as she stared into the youthful face of the person who meant so much to her in life.

"Even though I've been surrounded by many hot chicks and technically single, something was missing."

"What?"

Lee leaned forward and whispered, "You."

He brushed the hair away from her face and kissed her forehead. She could feel the intense heat from his lips and knew that everything was going to be fine.

"Are you ready for one more adventure?"

"Always," replied Brooke.

She smiled and took his hand.

Praise for Heaven's Casting Room

"Heaven's Casting Room is a playful labyrinthine adventure into a world of imaginative possibilities. Robert Dinning gives us a narrative redolent of Stefan Heym with its dalliance with the Infernal made flesh and the metaphysical made tangible. This is an arresting narrative."
- Steven O'Brien, The University of Portsmouth, UK

"Heaven's Casting Room is a romp, and a rant through a dream-like purgatory, where the tragic-comic hero, Balthazar, searches for redemption and meaning, and the answer to those eternal questions: who are we really, where are we going, and why? 'Here Comes Mr. Jordan' meets 'A Walk On The Wild Side'. 'Night-life of the Gods' mixes with 'Mean Streets'. A fantasy both whimsical and hard-edged."
-Thaddeus Hoople, London Bookseller and 30 year publishing veteran.

"In his latest novel, 'Heaven's Casting Room', Robert Dinning gives us an unfettered and real glimpse into the truth of life, complete with all of its harshness, beauty, pain, humour, anger and especially love. This is an excellent story."
- T. Anglen, Himmel Press

About the Author

Robert S. Dinning was born in Ontario in 1974. His love affair with the written word began as a child when his mother would read to him every night before bed. Before long, he was placing pen to paper and creating his own worlds. He received a Master's Degree in Creative Writing in 2001 and is currently completing a PhD. in the same field. When he is not writing, he can be found wandering in unusual places around the world, experiencing everything life has to offer.